I0451313

THE SHADOW COLLECTOR

TEMPORAL ARMISTICE BOOK 2

MATTHEW S. COX

DIVISION ZERO PRESS

The Shadow Collector
Temporal Armistice #2
© 2017 – Matthew S. Cox
All Rights Reserved

ISBN (ebook): 978-1-949174-74-8

ISBN (print): 978-1-949174-75-5

CONTENTS

1

DIRTY LAUNDRY

A nxiety has been leaving me pretty much alone for the past few days, but with a Monday off and nothing to do, I can't help but think about everything I've learned. This isn't the same little brain goblin that tormented me all my life. I don't have that constant worry something bad is right around the corner—like sitting at work wondering if I left the coffee maker on and I'm going to come home to a burned-out shell of an apartment building.

No, I think I killed him.

The goblin, I mean. I'm lying in bed, only a T-shirt on, staring at the ceiling, as I have been for the past few hours. Idleness has a new problem. Now I sit and try to wrap my brain around what I am. I mean, I guess I could freak the hell out and fall to bits, but what good would that do? Okay, so I'm not fully human. For most of my life, the nagging feeling I didn't quite belong constantly nibbled at my nerves. *Not* having that sense is a relief I can barely describe since I no longer *think* I'm an outsider—I *know*. I still *feel* mostly the same, other than the whole wings/tail/horns/strong-enough-to-lift-cars deal.

Usually, when I'm idle like this, the random thoughts would become unbearable. Hence why I wound up such a terror as a child. I always had to keep myself busy doing something. But that's past me.

So many thoughts and feelings I had over the years all make sense looking back on them. My present unease is purely rational, if unbelievable. I've potentially got the Mob watching me. I'm definitely stuck between two sides of an extradimensional war. And I might've made mortal enemies out of a mage's guild.

Oh, yeah... I'm also a demon.

Well, not technically. I'm part Shaar'Nath, which—according to my father—aren't demons. We're beings from another plane who happen to look quite a bit like what humans think of as demons. In fact, Dad believes humans invented the mythology after seeing our kind. Same goes for 'angels,' or Elestari. I snarl to myself. Pricks. So far, I've seen two of them, and one's a complete asshole. The other's a bit of a stuck-up priss, but maybe her heart's in the right place. I mean, she did help Lawrence.

Oh, there's also the little girl next door. Ashley. She's eight and her mother's not going to win any 'parent of the year' awards, but at least she's not an *active* threat to the kid. No, that title belonged to Frank, her *very* ex-boyfriend. The girl thinks she summoned me to protect her from that piece of shit. For once, the thin walls in this place did something good. I kicked in his door and stopped him before he could ruin that girl's entire life. She kinda knows what he almost did to her, but at the same time doesn't really understand. It's creepy how she believes she summoned me on purpose to kill him, knows I killed him, and is totally cool with it. So, yeah. Somehow I've pseudo-adopted my neighbor's daughter.

I've managed to figure out the constant unease shadowing me all my life came from sensing something wasn't quite right with me insofar as being normal goes. Honestly, I'm probably not freaking out because there's a lot about my reality that's pretty badass. Deep down, my subconscious mind must've sensed something different about me—beyond being telekinetic and having snow-white skin. With that horned cat out of the bag, silence no longer nudges me to the brink of a mental explosion. I can enjoy being bored for the first time in my twenty-three years.

Or I could, if I didn't have a whole bunch of *actual* worries to dwell on.

This 'being an adult' thing is way overrated. Though, to be fair, *normal* adults don't have these kinds of problems.

Blargh.

Okay, I have my own place, decent salary… being independent isn't all bad. I grew up poor. Some nights, a slice or two of bread or a bowl of rice wound up being dinner. Childhood isn't so much a nostalgic thing as it's me being lazy and missing a life before I had any responsibilities.

Though, a Monday off after my swing weekend at the fire department is pretty close to having no worries, at least for a bit. Pulling four twelves last week and going straight into back-to-back twelve-hour shifts on Saturday and Sunday as well completely sucks. There's no way around that. But, I get make-up time. Monday's a usual day off, and this week I get Tuesday and Wednesday on top of it.

I've decided not to apply for the permanent transfer to the Fire Marshal's Office. I'm young, not that experienced, and I don't have the necessary education to really be an arson investigator. I can coast a bit on my psychic abilities, but what really made the decision for me was the draw into the flames. Maybe it'll weaken in time and I'll change my mind, but at this point in my life, being at the front line feels right.

Captain Greene seemed a little disappointed, but cheered up when I offered to help with any arson investigation that involved magic or paranormal events. Nothing against her office, but I have a need to be right where I am. We did 'leave the door' open for the future, provided no mage with actual training in arson investigation gets the job before I change my mind. Not that I'm in a hurry. Dad thinks I'll live a few thousand years.

All my life, I've been the impulsive girl who leaps without looking, but for some reason, this time, I didn't. Maybe it's my practical side thinking since fire doesn't hurt me, it makes the most sense to be where that does the most good. I don't need any of the gear firefighters use. Guess if I ever let my secret fully out, I'd skip lugging all that stuff, but for now, I play normal.

Speaking of normal, I should probably get out of bed.

Some Elestari think I'm going to destroy the world and are no doubt watching my every move. There's even some Shaar'Nath doing that, too. About that whole destroying the world thing... I don't know too much about it other than being partially human could allow me to exploit some weakness that would end everything.

Well, not *everything*, just the human world.

This reality that holds Earth, the Solar System, and everything else out there is sitting in a dimension wedged between two others, separating the Shaar'Nath world from the Elestari's realm. After almost wiping each other out, members of both groups worked together to create this world as a forced armistice. They can't fight each other directly with the mortal realm acting as a physical barrier between them. Some (like my dad) even use the word Armistice as a name for the reality I've grown up in. Life here happened as an accident. Neither side intended to create humans (or anything else), but hey, shit happens. When you put together a fish tank and ignore it for ten thousand years, something you don't want's going to wind up growing in it.

I sit up and stare at my hands. My body appears to be human in every way except for my unnatural whiteness. A sly grin forms on my lips at the thought I can change that—appearing human I mean—at a whim.

With a groan, I peel my T-shirt off and trudge to the shower. Since discovering my nature, I've gotten in the habit of showering only with hot water. Come to think of it, I always did run the water on the warm side, even as a kid. Makes sense now why I've always felt cold when everyone else seemed comfortable.

So, yeah. I'm back to the normal firefighter routine, except for being on call with the FMO if they get a 'magic one.'

Since I'm in no hurry to be anywhere, I spend an inordinate amount of time luxuriating in the warmth and the feel of water pouring over me. I consider letting my wings out to give them a rinse, but this bathroom doesn't have anywhere near enough room for stretching out.

Once I've had enough, I dry myself off then chuck the towel over the shower curtain rail and pad across my apartment to the kitchen. Fixing myself breakfast doesn't require getting dressed. Hmm. Lost to indecision, I stand there for a minute or five staring at the cabinets with my hands on my hips. Do I want eggs, pancakes, cereal, or pizza rolls? More like: what do I want to clean up after?

"Hey," says Ashley, from behind.

My usual reaction to being startled is to freeze statue-still. It came in damn handy avoiding cops in my teen years. The human eye is drawn to motion, and freezing in place caused the cops to miss me more often than they'd like to admit. Once my shock wears off, I glance over my shoulder. My eight-year-old neighbor is lurking in the alcove between the kitchen and living room in a stained white T-shirt, a denim skirt with more than a few holes plus a mustard stain, and pink flip-flops. She's also evidently at ease with my standing here nude. Whoa. Awkward.

"Umm. How did you get in here?"

She looks up at me, eyebrows creeping together. "You gave me a key, remember? Are you still gonna watch me today?"

"Oh. Right." I rub my forehead, trying to wake up the rest of the way. "Yeah. Umm. Just got out of bed a few minutes ago and my brain's still asleep."

Ashley's stomach gurgles. She taps her right flip-flop into the floor. "It's okay. Mommy doesn't wear anything sometimes too 'cause she hates doing laundry."

I scurry off to my bedroom. "I'm not your mother."

After grabbing a clean black T-shirt and skirt, I return to find her standing exactly as I'd left her, wearing the same outfit she's had on for like the last nine days. In the months after our trailer burned, I had a pretty limited wardrobe too, so I know what it's like to be the kid stuck in the same shit for a whole week... or two.

I try to copy my mother's sympathetic smile, and pat her on the head. "Time for those clothes of yours to see the inside of a washing machine."

She shrugs. "Mom's gonna do wash tomorrow. It's okay. I wear the same stuff so she doesn't have to clean so much. It's probably 'cause she works at Starbucks. We don't have a lot of money and the machines are expensive."

"When I was your age, I had to wear the same stuff a lot too. My mother didn't mind doing the laundry, but she rarely had time or money. I had piles on my floor rated by how bad things smelled. After the fourth pile, it went in the hamper." I grin.

Ashley hops in a chair at the kitchen table, swinging her feet back and forth, smiling. "When I'm older, I'll do the wash for her so she doesn't have to."

Damn, that kid is too thin. I get pissed, but I really don't have a good target for my anger. Tracy, her mother, isn't completely at fault here. She's been dealt a bad hand. As long as she stays a lot more particular about the men she brings home, I don't have a real issue with her. Where these feelings of protectiveness toward the next-door kid came from, I haven't a clue. Does a summoning circle powered by strawberry syrup actually work? Could this kid have done some actual magic?

The noises coming out of her stomach are quite obvious, but I ask anyway.

"Did you eat breakfast yet? I was about to make something. Are you hungry?"

Ashley nods hard enough to make her hair dance. It's straight, long, and brown, almost down to the seat of the chair. Unlike her clothes, it looks clean. "If you're a demon, why did you 'grow up?' Aren't demons like... always big?"

Chuckling, I grab a pan and a bowl from the cabinets, and start making pancakes. "We're not really demons. My mother's a human, Dad's from the other side."

"Oh. I guess he didn't give your mom child sport."

I twist around to raise an eyebrow at her. "What?"

"Mommy says my daddy doesn't give her child sport 'cause he's got dead beets." Ashley keeps swinging her feet back and forth.

"Oh." I'm not sure if I should laugh or go break his legs. My mother's face appears in my thoughts with a disapproving frown. She'd tell me I can't solve everything with violence. "Sorry. My father wasn't around when I was little either."

"Were you a mistake too?" Ashley's dark brown eyes turn downward.

Aww. I abandon the batter in the bowl and move to the table, crouching beside her chair. No, I think I was very much on purpose... but not by either of my parents' intentions. "The mistake is that man not being a father to you. *You* are no mistake."

She looks up at me, her face somber, but at least she's not crying.

I take her hand. "My dad didn't show up when I was little because he'd been threatened by other creatures who said they'd hurt me if he didn't stay away."

Ashley scowls. "If he loved you, he'd have killed them before they could hurt you."

"I'm sure he thought about it... but those creatures are not easy to kill. They look like angels, but they're not. If he attacked them here, they'd only go back to where they came from. And he can't go there, so he would never know how many more might attack me."

She tilts her head. "Not angels? What are they?"

I ruffle her hair, grinning. "Buttheads."

Ashley laughs.

"For a long time, I thought my father was a bad person. I also thought I was human. When I discovered the truth on my own, he came to visit me."

Her smile fades. "Mine won't."

I poke her in the belly. "I never thought I'd see mine, and he showed up. Time can change people. Maybe someday, he'll realize what an idiot he's being. But, no matter what happens, it's not your fault."

"You sound like my mom."

"Well, in this case, she's right." I stand and resume stirring the batter. "I'm making pancakes, okay?"

Her grin returns, and she bounces. "Yay!"

I pour some batter in the pan and stand there watching the bubbles rise and burst. Tracy's been thinking of going to night school in hopes of getting a better job, and it can't be easy to make rent for her even in this crummy building. The idea of inviting her to move in with me as a roommate swirls around. These apartments have a small multipurpose room that could serve as a tiny bedroom, though they'd have to share it. I still haven't used it for anything more than storage. It wouldn't cost me anything but privacy to let them crash here, and take a huge financial burden off Tracy's back for a while.

Hmm.

I really wish I knew where all this protectiveness came from all of a sudden. Next-door neighbor's crummy life choices aren't my problem, but every time Ashley looks up at me with adoration, I crumble. Now I know how the cops felt whenever they picked me up. This kid's eyes aren't 'slightly oversized' like mine, but she can still crush me with guilt easily. I got away with so much shit by giving people 'that look,' and I really had done mischief.

A few minutes later, I'm sitting across the table, watching this kid inhale pancakes like she's never seen food before. I brush the roommate idea aside for now. Having my own place is nice, and I'm not sure Tracy would go for it. She might like privacy too. Besides, I have Jason now and well… thin walls are bad enough, but having them in the apartment with us?

"These are really good," says Ashley, right before stuffing another forkful in her mouth. A bead of syrup dribbles down her chin.

I tap the spot on my face and point at her. "Got some runaway maple."

She tries to lick it, but her tongue won't reach. Eventually, she wipes it with her hand and licks her fingers.

The roommate idea's a bit too much, too fast, but I can start smaller. "If you're ever hungry, you're welcome to eat here."

Ashley grins. "Okay. You're pretty cool for a demon."

Heh. Guess I'm not 'lame' anymore. Behold the power of sugar.

2

OUT OF THE CLOSET

My apartment's not exactly equipped for children. I don't have any toys, board games (do people even still play those?), or supplies for any of those 'fun activity to do with your kids' things that always seem to scroll by on Facebook. I still have no idea why I keep seeing that stuff. Seriously, if someone looked at my feed, they'd probably think I'm a middle-aged housewife with a litter of my own. Probably because I friended a bunch of fire-fighters and I don't post much.

Meh.

Fortunately, my inner child is an assertive bitch, so I have the *big* toy: a PlayStation 4. So what if it's not 'educational' or 'helping Ashley develop.' This girl needs some time to be a kid. And it's not like we're going to spend all day vegging on video games... only the eight or so hours Tracy needs to work.

Ashley cuddles against my side on the sofa, her legs curled under her, feet tucked in the gap between cushions. Though her attention remains locked on the little character she controls, she's made it a point to press herself into me since we started playing. I start to worry about how things are with her mother until I get a read on her intention. She feels safe with me, but I'm no replacement mom. That's another little perk of my nature. Usually, I can tell a person's intentions within a few seconds of looking at them. Probably how 'demons' in the old days could find a gullible idiot to take advantage of.

A few minutes past noon, my phone rings. Since reaching for it would require more effort than I'm prepared to invest at the moment, I nab it with a telekinetic tug, swipe to answer, and float it up to the side of my head.

"Hello?" I ask.

Ashley pauses the game to give me the wide eyes of 'that's *so* cool!' She's already asked me to teach her 'that magic' about a dozen times, and either doesn't grasp the concept of it being mental and not magical, or she thinks I'm trying to keep my 'demon secrets.'

"Brook? Where are you?" asks Natalie.

I nod to Ashley, who unpauses the game. "Home. On my sofa."

She sighs with a hint of whine. "You were supposed to be here for lunch. Are you still coming so we can work with that crystal?"

Shit. That's right. I forgot about that. "Umm. About that. I've got Ashley here."

"Oh," says Natalie. "That's cool. Can you bring her along?"

I bite my lower lip. Not that I'm worried about the kid seeing my true nature—that's already happened. Freakily enough, I didn't even scare her. In fact, I'm sure she thinks I'm 'cool.' Does that mean this kid is a little disturbed? Meh. Join the club. "Let me check with her mother. If Tracy's got no problem with it, we'll be there soon. Haven't eaten lunch yet anyway, we kinda got absorbed."

"Cool," says Natalie. "If you can make it, send me a text. If you can't, call me so I can hit you with a guilt hammer."

I laugh. "'Kay."

Ashley pauses the game again and looks up. "Who's that?"

"My friend Natalie."

"Oh, she sounded nice." Ashley tilts her head. "Did she ever fix your rune oven?"

Hah. Thin walls. "No, she's going to replace it. Thing's too far gone. I put instant ramen in there the other day and took out a bowl of scrambled eggs and chocolate syrup."

"Eww." She sticks her tongue out for a second. "I hate it when it does that. Ours keeps turning grilled cheese into marshmallow floof."

That's not *so* bad. People have floof sandwiches on purpose. Insane, damaged people… but they're still people. "Oh."

"With mustard," deadpans Ashley.

I shudder.

"So what's your friend want?"

"Before your mom asked if you could spend the day, I'd been planning to hang out with her."

Ashley fidgets with the controller. "Thank you for changing your plans for me."

"You're welcome. Besides, if your mom's okay with it, we can go visit my friend's store for a little while. She makes enchants."

"Really?" Ashley perks up so fast her head nearly flies off. "Can we?"

I dial Tracy's number. "Let me bounce it off your mother first."

My charge smirks. "Since when do demons have to ask permission?"

Since this particular demon with a shitload of juvenile arrests doesn't feel like getting charged with kidnapping as an adult. "I don't want to worry her."

"Hello?" asks Tracy, the din of a Starbucks going on behind her. "What's wrong?"

"Oh, nothing's wrong." I smile. "I forgot an errand I needed to run today. Do you mind if I bring Ash to Kensington for like an hour or two?"

"What kind of errand?"

"A friend of mine runs an enchanting shop over there, and she wanted my help with something. It's not super important. I can reschedule if you're worried about Ash."

"The macchiato's supposed to be a grande, not a venti," yells Tracy. "Sorry. Umm. Sure, okay. You know I can't afford it if she breaks something."

"No worries… I broke a lot of shit my mother couldn't pay for as a kid."

Tracy mumbles something about the drive-through before coming back to the phone. "It's not dangerous, is it? I mean nothing you can't deal with?"

"Probably safer than being in that Starbucks from the sound of it."

"Ugh. Wall to wall," mumbles Tracy. "Okay, I gotta go."

I grin at the kid. "Later."

Ashley bounces up and down. "What'd she say?"

"Get your flip-flops on."

"Yay!" she squeals, fists thrust into the air over her head.

We leave the game paused. Ashley zooms for the kitchen to collect her footwear while I hit the bedroom to add combat boots to my T-shirt and skirt ensemble. I briefly entertain the idea of flying there, but it's still broad daylight. Guess it's Uber time again. One of these days, I really should get a car. Lieutenant Sims, my boss, mentions that at least twice a week. He came up with a new parry for my usual question of 'is the department paying for it' Thursday by saying 'yes, technically, since we pay your salary.'

Wiseass.

I've never owned a car before, though I have driven. First time behind the wheel, I was about eight, wearing my nightgown (one of Mom's old T-shirts), and wanted ice cream in a major way before she woke up. Mom did *not* find it anywhere near as fun as I did. When I was fifteen, I drove her home from work once or twice when she was so exhausted she'd count as drunk. Got lucky there; the cops didn't pull us over.

Oh, crap. I should probably get a license before I buy a car, right? They won't even sell me one without that. Or, is it, they won't let me have insurance? Or is the law that I can't buy a car without insurance? Grr. Why do people have to make traveling so complicated? There's another reason I should keep my wings secret—someone'll make me buy insurance.

Ashley stands by the front door, waiting. After paging an Uber, I lead the way into the hall and lock my door. She takes my hand, probably something her mother insists on, and we head down to street level to wait for the car.

A pack of guys clustered by the wall of the building across the street look our way, over the roof of a fluorescent green Toyota that's been modded to ridiculousness. That poor car has such little ground clearance, a pubic hair would hit it like a speed bump. The guys wave, whistle, and catcall me, a mix of English and Spanish. Ashley's quiet sigh and eye roll tells me she's used to hearing the same garbage when her mother gets it.

I glance over the shitheads, feeling out their intent. Since none of them throw off vibes like they're going to do anything more than be annoying, I ignore them. A few minutes pass of them muttering amongst one another, no doubt discussing what they think they'd do with me in the bedroom for a while. The biggest guy among them keeps swatting at the others whenever they get too close to the car. Heh. It's his. Why is it the huge dudes always have the teeny cars?

"Hey, Mommy," calls one in Spanish. "You got a fine ass. Why don' we leave the kid wit' my sister and I show you the right way to love." He grabs his crotch. "I got so much for that pussy of yours right here, you won't be walkin' right for a week."

Oh, that's charming.

"*Mamacita?*" whispers Ashley. "Does he think you're my mother? That means 'mom', right? What did he say?"

"He said my hair looks nice and I have a cute daughter."

Ashley smirks. "I think you're making that up."

Prince Charming's beer bottle flies out of his hand and smashes through the windshield of the little car. Maybe I moved his arm just a wee bit so it looks like he threw it.

"Hey, man, what the fuck!" shouts the big guy, right before pulling a knife.

Oops.

Ashley gasps.

The idiot completely forgets I exist and stammers at his friend, repeating 'the fuckin' thing just flew' about ten times in rapid Spanish. No one pulls a gun, but I still put myself between them and Ashley. She clings, peering around my side at the men forming up for a brawl.

Luckily, our ride, a black Nissan sedan, shows up before anything more than shouting happens. Perfect timing.

THE UBER DROPS US OFF IN FRONT OF NATALIE'S SHOP, 'ENCHANTED Evenings,' after a brief and uneventful trip. Our driver wasn't a talker, and spent the whole time wearing headphones with Indian music turned up so loud, I could've followed along if I understood the language.

Ashley drags me across the sidewalk to the window and stares in awe at the display of animated ten-inch dolls walking around in a scale model of a Victorian London street. She watches them for a minute or two before looking up at me with saucer eyes.

"They're moving!" she half-whispers.

I grin. "Yeah. They're enchanted."

"Are they like people?" She resumes gawking at the window. A fog patch spreads out from her face along the glass.

"No, more like robots. They're not alive or anything."

"Oh. They're so pretty." She grins.

As soon as I approach the door, it swings itself open, a chime of ghostly bell tones accompanying it, though no physical source for the melody exists. Ashley looks up and around, dutifully hanging on to my hand. The second she sees the little walled-off area to the right of the entrance full of toys, she's off like a shot. A pair of massive floor-to-ceiling shelves converge at an angle, enclosing a space set up as a playroom. It's kinda like the 'keep the kids occupied' room in a car dealership, but stuff here moves on its own.

Ashley darts past the gate and steps over the tracks of a carved wooden train chugging around in a figure eight. Her attention goes straight to a shelf full of faerie dolls.

"Hey you!" Natalie trots over. "Wow. Someone really is trusting you with their offspring."

I fold my arms, a wry smile curling my black-painted lips. "This one's mother was too naïve. You got the oven ready? What about the seasonings?"

Ashley's head peers up over the gate. She gives me a flat look for a second or two, sticks out her tongue with a raspberry, and sinks down out of sight.

"I like her." Natalie points at the toy trove and laughs.

She pops up again holding a faerie with glowing, gossamer wings. "Can I play with stuff here?"

I point at Natalie. "Her call."

"Sure." She waves at the child. "Be careful with the dollhouse."

"Okay," chimes Ashley from out of sight behind the wooden gate.

"Stay in the play area, okay?" I lean up on tiptoe, trying to hurl my voice over the barrier.

"I will," replies Ashley.

Natalie leads me over to the counter, where she's already got the Aznian crystal sitting atop a little plate about the size of a DVD, made of dark grey stone flecked with reflective black specks. At present, the potato-sized hunk of crystal looks as clear as glass. My friend hovers over it with a barely contained expression of anticipatory glee.

She loves learning stuff.

You know that kid in school who's always got her nose in a book and never goes to parties unless her friends duct tape her up and dump her in a clothes hamper? Yeah, that's Natalie. Though she's mellowed to the party thing. Or at least the going-out-to-eat-a-couple-times-a-month thing. Since we're done with college, there hasn't been much partying going on.

"Nat…" I lean on the counter, staring at the crystal. "We've known each other for a while now, right?"

"Yeah." She grins for a few seconds before a look of concern flattens her lips. "Is something wrong?"

"No… at least I don't think so. I'm still the same person you met in Quincy Hall."

Natalie blinks. "Oh, holy crap!"

"Calm down. It's not that big a deal. I don't feel right going any longer without trusting you with something. You're my best... my only *real* friend, and you have to know."

She lurches across the counter and hugs me. "Oh, that's awesome! It's cool if you're gay. It changes nothing." Natalie lets gravity drag her back across the counter until we make eye contact.

Okay, I figured she'd jump to that conclusion. "It's not that. It's a little more complicated."

"Oh." She leans closer and whispers, "Are you like, in love with me?"

I sigh. "Yeah, you got me. Get those pants off right now."

"You're not serious." She laughs.

"Maybe with enough alcohol." Guess I know why it takes so much to get me smashed now. "Look, Nat. I need you to understand that there's something about me that's really hard to explain and maybe a little frightening."

"You have a dick?"

I frown. We dormed together and I have a pretty casual relationship with clothing. "You know that's not true."

She cackles. "Yeah, but your face."

It's nearly impossible not to inherit Natalie's giggles. Once I manage to calm enough to put on a serious expression, I pull my T-shirt off, exposing a racerback athletic top.

Natalie leans back, both eyebrows up and a hint of blush in her cheeks. "Oh, I thought you were kidding about that."

"You brought up the gay thing. And honestly, *that* would be so much easier to tell you—it's just another form of love. Nat... I'm not what you think I am. Hell. I'm not what I spent my whole life thinking I am."

"Just show her already," yells Ashley.

Natalie glances at the play area. "Wait, you told some random kid something you're having this much trouble spitting out to me?"

"She found out by accident." I lean close and whisper, "Didn't mean to. Some creep was about to umm... yeah."

"Did you brain-explode him too?" Natalie sends an 'aww' look at the play area.

"Not exactly, but the end result was the same." I take a step back. "Please don't hate me."

Natalie leans on the counter. "Are you planning to backstab me, burn down my shop, or do something really scummy and shitty to me?"

"No, never." My eyebrows scrunch together.

She beams. "Well then, out with it."

"Go on, *do* it," yells Ashley, still out of sight behind the gate.

"What if I told you that everything you know about demons is wrong?"

Natalie giggles. "You do a really lousy Laurence Fishburne."

Sue me. I'm female. My voice can't go there. "I'm serious."

"Like… no… You're possessed?"

"Wow, for the Girl Who Reads, you're missing the obvious," I say.

Ashley peers up over the gate, raising her hands in a pantomime of a wizard. "Minion, reveal yourself!"

I crack up laughing.

Natalie grins but looks back and forth between me and the kid like she's missing the joke. Well, I guess she is.

"Nat, please don't freak out."

She takes my hand. "Brook. Whatever you're going to do, stop torturing yourself and tell me."

"I'm not fully human. That's why the Aznian crystal changed color." I put my hand on it, making it glow bright crimson. "Oh well, might as well show you."

Natalie gestures at the lit up stone while muttering some incantation that causes two counter-rotating rings of yellow energy to appear over the counter. Mystical sigils squiggle into being, as if an invisible brush wrote in the air with light. "Ooh. This crystal isn't enchanted. It's reacting to some kind of energy in you."

I let my wings out.

My friend looks up at the leathery *fwoof* noise, and her jaw hangs open. "You have wings…"

Wow, this is more awkward than when the police made me confess to my mother the first time I got high. Maybe I overstated how much pressure it took to get me to try peyote, and maybe my slightly-too-large eyes helped convince everyone I was a manipulated innocent. "Yep. That's only part of it." You know, it's interesting that the peyote hit me hard but alcohol's like water.

She stands up. "You're like seriously a demon?"

"No. I just play one on TV."

Natalie blinks. "What'chu talkin' 'bout, Lucy?"

I snicker, making my wings shake. A fast-moving bit of bright pink-purple light catches my eye. One of the faerie dolls is flying around in circles near the ceiling, its wings aglow. Oh, whew. Nothing dangerous. "One sec."

I kick off my boots and slide my panties out from under my skirt. No sense ruining them.

Natalie raises an eyebrow.

Out come the horns, tail, glowing eyes, and claws. All twenty of them. I open my mouth. "Fangs too."

"Holy shit."

"Yeah," I say, "That's about the same reaction I had, only with more flying into the side of a building involved."

"Umm." She stares at me.

I've never adored my special talent as much as I do at that moment. While Natalie's body language is impossible to read and her facial expression is going into terrifying 'get away from me' territory, the psychic impression I get from her is pure 'OMG – I must study this!' She's thrilled and about to faint from excitement.

Shit.

After pulling all my extra bits back in, I rush around the counter and grab her before she passes out. She paws and pokes at me while giggling in a manic high-pitched squeal. This soon becomes bouncing and hugging like we won the lottery or something. Realizing she's not going to run off screaming, and doesn't hate me, I hug the shit out of her.

Eventually, I'm dressed again and we're sitting on a pair of minia-ture sofas in the 'books' section of the store. Ashley's low muttering emanates from the play area in a continuous chatter. Oh, hell. There's no way I'm getting her out of here without buying her at least a small enchanted toy.

"Nat, how much are those little faerie thingees?" I ask.

"Those?" She scrunches up her nose. "I made them so long ago… You know, I once had a little boy about her age want one." Natalie rolls her eyes with a sigh. "The kid's mother flipped out about 'boy toys' and 'girl toys' and threw a fit about her son asking for a faerie. Demanded I make an Army helicopter or something that flew the same way."

"Poor kid." I shake my head. "What's wrong with some people?"

Natalie winks. "Oh, it had a happy ending. The kid's father—who by the way looked like a biker—bought it for him. Little guy was over the moon. So…" She leans closer and whispers, "What happened to her?"

I sigh and lean forward before giving her the short version in a low voice. She doesn't need to know all the grisly details, only that Frank got a nice close look at my claws. "He would've seriously hurt her."

Natalie peers up at me with the meekest expression I've ever seen on her and whispers, "You… killed someone?"

"If you want to get technical, using the word 'someone' confers humanity on that slug. And hey, you knew about the guy when I was a kid. Besides. I didn't actually do that. So technically, my kill count is still the same. One perv out of the gene pool." Hmm. I suppose I did redirect that other idiot's gun to his own head. So I'm improving the average intelligence of the human gene pool by two.

"You didn't?" She blinks. "And normal people don't track 'kill counts.'"

I roll my eyes. "Normal people don't have horns either."

She purses her lips. "Fair point. So, the creep who tried to grab you? Someone else gave him a fatal nosebleed?"

Oh, this is going to take a while. By the time I'm done explaining my dad, the reason he didn't show up during my childhood, the whole Armistice thing, and how two races of extraplanar creatures inspired a large part of human mythology vis-à-vis angels and demons, Ashley's launched twelve faeries. Multicolored streams of light zip and glide all over the store. A sudden, high-pitched cheer gets me to snap my head around and stare at her hanging off one of the book-shelf walls of the play area, about midway up the second story.

Crap!

"Ash! What are you doing?" I leap to my feet and face her.

"Faerie's stuck in the books," yells the kid.

When she twists to look at me, she loses her grip and falls, but I catch her with telekinesis. Natalie starts to scream, but realizes I'm making her float and melts with relief.

Ashley waves her arms and legs while hanging in midair. "Whoa! This is cool!"

I set her down gently on her feet. "Please don't climb stuff."

"But the faerie's stuck." She looks terrified of getting in trouble.

"Sec," I mutter to Natalie before jogging to the front of the store to retrieve the faerie. Once it's airborne again, I usher Ashley back into the playroom and return to my seat. "Thing flew headfirst into the shelf. Is there a way to control them?"

"Yeah. Each one has a ring... should be on its display stand. If she puts the ring on, that faerie will go wherever she wants. If no one wears the control ring, they glide around randomly."

I head back to the gate, relay the instructions regarding the rings, and ask her to put them all back on their stands when she's done playing.

"Okay." Ashley nods.

Yet again, I jog across the store, flop on the sofa, and exhale. "Wow. Kids are tiring."

"So..." Natalie grins while pointing her pen at me. "Do you like get pregnant the normal way, or do you have to summon them?"

I stick my tongue out. "Summoning doesn't work."

"But..."

"Dad says Shaar'Nath know if a human tries to summon them, speaking their true name. They show up if they want to."

"Oh." She jots something in her notebook. "So if someone speaks your true name, you'll know they're doing it?"

"Yeah," I say.

"Hi!" shouts Ashley, right behind me.

I go stone-still as my muscles lock up.

She holds up an ordinary-looking red ball. "Look at this thing!"

My heart starts beating again.

Ashley drops the ball, which proceeds to bounce again and again without losing height. "It's a forever bouncer."

"Wow… that's kinda cool." My head bobs up and down, following it.

"This place is awesome!" Ashley nabs the ball and runs back to the toy area.

Natalie leans close. "Lemme see your hand?"

I hold it out. "What's up? Reading my fortune?"

She grabs my wrist and twists my arm palm-up before throwing her head back, her other hand pressed to her forehead. "I sense a great amount of weirdness in your future."

We both laugh.

"Seriously… just a couple of detection spells," says Natalie.

During the few minutes I endure her muttering and random glowing clouds of mist forming around my hand, a faint doorbell chime goes off near the front. No one walks in, so I ignore it.

"Hmm. No magic running on you, but I'm detecting a pile of energy inside you that I've never seen before."

"Gee, I wonder what that could be?" I roll my eyes.

She chuckles.

"Thanks for not flipping out on me."

Natalie makes a silly face while shrugging. "No biggie. It's not like you changed at all, you've always been who you are. The whole Frank thing is more unnerving, but I can see why you did that. Guess I should try not to like make you insanely pissed off, huh?"

"You couldn't possibly get me that pissed off."

She play-frowns. "I am a little jealous that you're going to live so long. When I'm getting old, maybe I'll transfer my consciousness into an urn or something so I can pester you for eternity."

I'm not sure if I should laugh or go crawl into a dark place some-where. "Wow… Fuck. I never thought about that." Realizing Nat's going to die and I'm probably not going to look any different at that point is like a fist to the gut. It takes me a lot of focus not to break down and cry right there.

"Oh, storing consciousness isn't *that* difficult. I should have it figured out by then." She winks.

"Heh. Speaking of enchantments… Umm… I was wondering if you might be able to whip something up for me. It's kinda irritating to burst out of my clothes when I go all the way."

Natalie's eyebrows go up. "All the way?"

"Yeah. I think of it like 'fully shifting.' I get these armor plates and I'm like seven feet tall. Usually rips my crap right off."

"Hmm." She snaps her fingers. "I got it! I'll make you a ring—no, that'll break when you get bigger. An amulet! I'll make you an amulet that creates an illusion of clothes… for emergencies."

I perk up. "You can do that?"

"Sveetie, I can do anyzthing."

"Except for whatever accent that was supposed to be."

We crack up laughing again.

Something tugs on my bootlace, and there's a tiny chirp from low to the ground.

I look down at a severely miniature Ashley, like if a Barbie doll had an eight-year-old daughter. "Holy shit! What happened?"

She looks up at us, hyperventilating and panicky.

Natalie loses it, and laughs so hard tears stream out of her eyes.

"Nat…" I scoop Ashley up like a pet mouse. She trembles, curls up in a ball on my palm, and refuses to look down at the floor as I stand back up. "Nat!"

My friend holds up a 'wait a minute' finger while trying to rein in her giggles.

"It's not funny!" squeaks Ashley.

Alas, the minuscule voice triggers another fit of laughter from Natalie.

I cuddle the kid in two hands, and absentmindedly pet her head with one finger.

"I'm not a hamster!" shouts Ashley.

Natalie falls off the sofa, pounding her fist into the floor, completely lost to laughter.

"What happened?" I whisper.

Sniffling, Ashley points toward the toy area and wails, "I don't know! The world got big!"

"Nat, please. She's terrified."

Still snickering, Natalie pushes herself up to kneel. "She rang the doorbell on the dollhouse. It's fine. Come on."

We follow her across the store. Natalie pulls open the gate to the play area for me, and I step over the still-running wooden train set. The back end of the enclosed section is home to an enormous three-story wooden doll mansion. A normal-sized engraved bronze doorbell plate next to the door glows with a soft, golden light.

Natalie points at the house. "Set her down there. It's a shrink enchant so kids can play inside the dollhouse. Ring the doorbell again and it will stop."

Ashley hangs her head. "I'm sorry."

"It's all right." I set her down.

It takes her using both hands to push the button far enough in to make it work. As soon as the soft *ding dong* echoes from inside the house, the doorbell plate ceases glowing and Ashley sprouts back up to normal size, two orange wisps of energy spiraling around her. She gazes at her hands in awe for a second before grabbing on to me and shivering. Little too much magic too fast, I think.

"You okay?" I ask.

Ashley nods, and lets out a heavy breath. "Yeah. That was freaky."

"You guys eat yet?" asks Natalie, in a not-terribly-transparent attempt at changing the subject.

"Nope." I shake my head.

"Pizza, Mexican, or Chinese?" Natalie swings her hand around; the instant her palm faces up, her cell phone appears. "They're the only delivery options around here."

"I'm okay with anything... Ash?"

She bounces. "Pizza!"

"Done." Natalie winks.

3

SUCCUBUS

My revelation to my best friend went better than I expected, and Ashley made out like a bandit. I got her one of those flying faerie dolls (she chose purple wings) and Nat, in addition to giving her the ball that doesn't lose energy when it bounces, only charged $50 for the doll after I insisted we couldn't simply take it. I suspect they're pricier than that, but as long as I've been visiting there, I've never noticed anyone buy toys. Either that or she replaces them easily whenever someone takes one.

Tracy had mixed feelings about the gift, since she can't afford that sort of thing. I assured her I wasn't trying to 'steal' her kid, and knew all about being dirt-ass poor. Her desperation radiated a bit more than I felt comfortable with. While her intent didn't have a specific focus, it sorta kinda got me worried she might do something dangerous for easy money. I left with telling her to ask me if she needs help, and not to do anything that'll orphan her daughter.

I think that left a mark.

So… Tuesday. Jason calls me around two in the afternoon. I'm watching Ashley again, but we make plans to go out at six, once the kid is home with her mother. The day's quietly wasted on video games and delivery subs.

Jason shows up at 5:30 p.m., right when I'm in the middle of fixing Ashley something to eat since I'm going out for dinner. Her mother will probably give her a cheese sandwich or something, so I toss a pair of hot dogs in the rune oven and run to get the door. Jason's in the hall in a long, dark coat, a broad smile making his chest-long red beard a little wider.

"Hey," he says. "Missed you."

I grin. "I haven't gone anywhere. Swing plus days off."

"Ugh. I'm up week after next." He stuffs his hands in his pockets and sighs while stepping inside.

His overacted dread is kinda cute.

Ashley screams.

I whirl to face the kitchen at the same instant a *bang* comes from the table. A haze of lime-hued smoke lingers for a few seconds, clearing to reveal a splatter of transparent green slime covering Ashley (and the table, walls, and ceiling). She sits frozen in place, one arm extended over the plate, a knife still pressed down where she'd evidently attempted to cut a piece off a hot dog.

She pivots her goop-covered face toward me. A blob drops from her cheek onto the plate and quivers. "Your rune oven *sucks*."

Fighting the urge to laugh, I grab some paper towels and clean her up. Fortunately, the slime has the consistency of semi-dried snot and doesn't soak into her clothes. After rolling it up into a wad, I chuck it in the trash. The other hot dog didn't burst, but it smells like raspberry. Uh, no. Out it goes. Jason peels splats off the walls and ceiling while I conduct a second attempt exposing hot dogs to the rune oven from hell. I hit the orange gem this time, which produces warm hot dogs that still smell (and behave) like hot dogs.

Ashley's suspicious at first, but after a few exploratory fork pokes, she digs in.

Tracy's home by 6:18. After apologizing for being late and thanking me profusely for watching Ash again, they head home, one apartment away. As soon as the door closes, I wrap my arms around Jason from behind.

"So, what did you have in mind?" I coo. "Dinner, movie, and dancing, or did you want to practice some hose drills later?"

He pats my hands while swaying side to side. "I think tonight might be the most amazing night of my life."

Oh wow. He wants me to be happy. I mean, yeah sure, there's a definite undercurrent of 'Yay! Sex!' in there—I mean, he *is* a guy—but it's not drowning out that he wants me to be happy. I almost don't know how to process that, since it's the first time I've ever had a man throw off those particular vibes. Usually they give off something between their genuine expectation that they're going to be 'the best I've ever had' or the 'Yay! Sex!' thing.

Jason spins around. We stand in my living room kissing for a while before my stomach gets pissed off. I nibble perhaps a skosh too hard on his lip and wink.

"Hungry?" he asks.

Innocent face. "Whatever gave you that idea?"

"Were you planning to go out like that?"

I stare down at my T-shirt, sweatpants, and black-painted toenails. "I guess this is a little too casual."

Once I change into a black T-shirt, jeans, and Doc Martens, and load up on cheap bracelets, we're out the door. That little green Toyota hasn't been back since I put a Bud Light through its windshield, and for that matter, neither have those guys. Wonder how nasty that fight got? Oh well. The neighborhood is poorer for their absence.

Jason's truck is pretty big, and it's such a cool feeling not to have to use public transportation for once. Yeah, maybe I should get my own car. Fire department pay isn't exactly astounding, but it's decent... and I live in a hellhole. Hah. By the way, Dad thought my living in Apartment 66 on the sixth floor was hilarious.

Jason drives to this upper-end-of-middle Portuguese restaurant that makes me feel underdressed. A small army of three-foot marble gladiator statues lines a walkway along the front of the building from the parking lot to the door. About half of them are enchanted to move, brandishing their weapons at each other. Everyone else in the waiting area (and Jason) looks like we should be going to a formal event or something. Button-down shirts, slacks, and fancy dresses are everywhere. I'm the only tool in a T-shirt and jeans. Oops. I wish he would've said something, but fuck it… we're here.

A painting of some old-timey man in the waiting area shifts its gaze to me and frowns, no doubt offended by my 'common' attire. I flip the painting off, kissing the tip of my middle finger. The man gasps, though it makes no sound. After that, he makes it a point not to look in my direction.

No one alive comments on my clothes, and we soon have a nice, quiet booth table surrounded by ivy-covered wooden lattice. It's probably plastic ivy, but it looks cool. Illusory fireflies glide around the leaves, aglow in blue, green, and yellow. The candles are a nice touch. Jason orders a bottle of wine, which of course gets me carded. Sigh. A bit of my teen surliness appears on my face while I flash my ID. I'm not old enough for that to be a compliment. At least our waiter doesn't give me the 'I'm sure that's fake but I can't prove it' sneer. He nods and takes the request for a drink without further protest.

We spend a few minutes perusing the menus, and I wind up picking an entrée with rice, clams, mussels, shrimp, and mushrooms. Jason gets a slab of fish you could legit knock someone out with. Seriously, it's over an inch thick and wider than his hand span.

Speaking of which, the contents of my bowl could've fed me and Mom dinner twice back in the day. Yeah, maybe two-thirds of this is coming home with me. We take our time with the food while our conversation wanders around everything from the fire department, to video games, to what else we do for fun. He shies away from talking too much about his past, but does open up enough to tell me his mother died a few years ago from cancer and his father moved to one of those condo developments for the fifty-five plus crowd, though the two haven't spoken in years. Jason moved back into his childhood home after his mother passed.

"That's kinda cool, I guess. Not many people our age have houses." I swirl my fork around the rice/seafood mixture. Delicate conversations aren't my strong point. Saying whatever the hell I think works better for me, that whole impulsive thing. "Sorry your dad's an asshole." Oops. There that is. Though, he really ought to see the real me.

"Eh, don't be. *He* isn't sorry." Jason takes a glug of wine before smiling at me. "I try not to talk about him because it gets me angry. They divorced the year I turned ten. She got the house. Guess that finally made him realize he fucked up. It wound up working better for both of us, I think. Only being around him for a couple hours at a shot when he hadn't been loaded was different."

I nod. "Sorry. No frame of reference here. My dad is out of this world."

He almost chokes on a forkful of rice and rushes to get a napkin over his mouth. "Gah." He coughs twice. "I wasn't ready for that."

"Yeah. Neither was I." The food here is really damn good. I've got to bring Nat here the next time we go out. "I made a bunch of assumptions about him, and the first time we met, I hit him square in the face."

Jason's eyebrows shoot up, but he's chewing, so he doesn't try to speak.

"Mom never talked about him. No photos. Whenever I asked her anything related to Dad, she'd get spacey…"

"Ahh. Yeah. I can understand where that would lead you." He smiles. "Glad to hear it wasn't."

I chuckle. "Yeah, the truth is way more out there."

We drift back into talking about the fire department and how we both wound up there. For him, he applied on a whim since it was 'a job.' It still takes a certain kinda person to even entertain the idea of such a potentially dangerous career, but he's stuck with it ever since he'd been eighteen. Not the 'life calling' situation like me, but he's dedicated enough to keep at it. That gets us onto the subject of me plus fire. While we nurse our post-dinner coffee and await our take-home boxes, I tell him the story of Mom's house trailer burning down when I was twelve. Why the details blanked out of my memory for so long, I have no idea, though…

I have a suspicion.

Those damn Elestari. They threatened to kill me if Dad showed himself to me before I 'found out on my own' what I am, and I bet they figured me discovering that fire couldn't hurt me at twelve was a little too early for their grand scheme. Wonder if Natalie could tell if I'd been enchanted to forget. Suppose it doesn't matter anymore since I remember. Not like it would change anything to learn the Elestari made me forget. At the time, I'd been a kid, and sometimes, kids blank out scary shit.

Right now, however, a burning trailer is the last thing on my mind. I lean over the table, grab hold of his bright red beard, and pull him into a kiss. His dark hazel eyes widen in surprise for an instant before half-lidding. He tries to tug back at the approach of rustling plastic bags, but I don't let go, and continue kissing him as the waiter leaves our food and the check on the edge of the table.

"Get a room," mutters a woman two tables over, probably not expecting me to overhear.

"How petty should I be?" I whisper.

Between kisses, Jason asks, "What are you thinking?"

"That foo-foo drink looks top-heavy." I shift my eyes to the right, honing in on this giant blue-and-green goblet. "Might fall into her lap."

"Funny as that would be, someone will get stuck cleaning that up." Jason kisses me again.

He's got a point. Her ice water topples into her lap with a little help from yours truly.

The shrieking banshee kills the mood, but at least she gives us a laugh leaping to her feet and swatting at her dress with a napkin. Her son, who's maybe six, finds this as hilarious as I do. Waiters rush over to help, and amid the confusion, Jason takes care of the bill.

Well, that was exciting.

I'M CERTAIN THE LAST TIME I WAS IN A MOVIE THEATER, TWO THINGS HAD been true: I didn't have boobs yet, and I didn't pay to get in. Telekinesis opened up a whole wide world of mischief. Whether getting past locked doors or knocking crap over as a distant distraction, I exploited the shit out of it. This is also the first time I've ever held the concept of romance and a movie theater in my brain at the same time. None of the guys I hung out with from fifteen upward really did the 'dating' thing. We usually loitered around and did stupid shit, or drank and then did stupider shit.

Being in a theater on a date, *and* paying to get in… weird. Are we supposed to watch the movie or is it just a way to be in a dark room with him? We wind up deciding on some Marvel superhero flick. I've never been a *huge* fan of comic books, but I don't dislike them. These kinds of movies are okay in a flashy colors and explodey way. The guy in the red suit is my kind of wiseass anyway. Ha. I didn't think super-hero movies would have this much blood in them. Okay, maybe I *could* get interested in this shit.

It's adorable. Jason, I mean, not the movie. We hold hands and kiss on and off. I get a few dirty looks when decapitations or people getting squished make me laugh out loud. By the time it's over, I think I understand why the whole 'dinner and a movie' thing happened. Food needs time to settle. The 'dinner and straight to sex' thing would likely require changing the bedding and probably a carpet steamer rental.

Figure I'm good to go when we get back to the truck and the over-powering smell of Portuguese seafood triggers a little hunger.

Once we climb in and close the doors, he reaches over and takes my hand. "So…"

"So yourself." I grin. "And don't tell me you're going to change your mind now. I've been waiting all night."

His smile is large and tinged with a hint of hesitation. "Not at all. If you aren't."

I shake my head rather emphatically, grinning.

Jason's wags his eyebrows at me. "Would you rather head back to your place or see the house?"

I rub my chin. "That depends on how much you want anywhere from six to ten people hearing everything we do."

Jason laughs. "My place then… It's a row house, but the between walls are pretty thick."

"Sounds good."

———

A LITTLE PAST 10:30 P.M., JASON PARKS ON WEBSTER STREET IN COBBS Creek, in front of a solid block of row houses. His has a round balcony on the second floor with a bright green roof. It doesn't look big on the outside, but it's probably deep. He unlocks the front door and pulls it open for me.

It's definitely a bachelor pad. The dining room table's not been used for anything but storing old pizza boxes for a while. His PS4 is set up in the living room like a Shinto shrine on a tiny table in front of the TV, and the couch has seen better days. Probably the same sofa that's been here for thirty years.

"Nice place… It's cozy."

"That means small." He chuckles. "Eh, what do I need much room for?"

We flop on the couch after he gets some iced tea from the fridge. I remember him saying his dad plus beer equaled badness, so I don't comment on the lack of alcohol. Really, I drank enough from fifteen to nineteen to scratch that itch.

After fifteen minutes of easy conversation, it becomes quite clear he's not going to make the first move. I scoot closer and throw my leg over, sitting in his lap facing him. He wants to make love to me, but he's also worrying about doing the wrong thing and ruining what we've got going on between us.

Wow… that's a new feeling for me.

I start by kissing him on the lips and move down to his neck, tossing around the idea of maybe giving him a mark he'll have fun explaining tomorrow. His hands roam my body, and we get the same idea at the same time. He goes for my belt while I go for his. Clothes peel away, item by item, with lots of writhing, kissing, and squeezing going on between. Eventually, we're both in nothing but our underpants.

He's quite obviously ready. I scratch at his length through the fabric, causing him to arch his back and clench his jaw while sucking air between his teeth.

"Careful, I bite." I lean in and kiss him on the chest before nibbling on his nipple.

His long, low groan washes over my hair with a hot breath. When he stretches out to lie flat on the sofa, I climb up and straddle him. Jason's manhood is about to tear its way out of his boxers. He traces his hands down my sides, snagging my panties and tugging them over my hips.

A wicked grin curls my lips as I let my tail out and slip the ten-inch blade gingerly between his leg and underwear. The tension that locks his muscles turns me on a little when he sees it. I angle the edge up and slice the fabric. Jason bursts out of his boxers, but makes a high-pitched gasp, his eyes bulging.

Okay, he wasn't lying about not being bothered by what I am at least. Seeing the tail hasn't had any, umm, 'softening' effect.

"Uhh…" He flashes a nervous grin. "You're not like going to drain my life or anything?"

I arch my back, letting my horns, wings, and claws out to play. My growing smile seems to frighten and excite him at the same time. "Like a succubus?"

"Something like that, yeah…"

Careful not to cut him, I trace all ten fingernails over his skin from shoulder to the base of his manhood. He makes the cutest little noise somewhere between a squeak of alarm and arousal. Before an accident happens, I retract the claws. If my tail can cut steel, they probably can, too. "You know, I have no idea…" Arms folded, I tap one finger at my chin. "Nothing like that's ever happened before. But they say succubi devour souls, and you're a ginger—you should be safe."

He grins. "All right then."

My little devilish moment gone, I hide my wings so I don't tear down his house as we writhe and roll around. It doesn't take long for us to fall off the sofa to the carpet. Jason spends a while circling my nipples with his tongue, and yeah, it's a good thing his house has thicker walls. No one has ever made me make that noise before.

He kisses my neck; I nibble on his shoulder, raking scratches across his back with normal fingernails. Jason nudges me closer and closer to the edge with his hands and tongue, kissing down my front until his lips are south of my navel, but not south enough. A loud moan leaks from my throat as my back arches and I grab at the carpet. I try to slide back to get his mouth where I want it, but he lifts his head away and winks.

"I… I'm…" I gasp. "Almost… stop teasing me." I snarl into his ear.

"You are the best thing that's ever happened to me." He reaches for the lump of jeans on the floor and pulls a little foil packet out of the back pocket.

Wow… a condom. Usually, the guys I wind up with don't bother. Not like I've ever had any real urge to like be sensible or anything. With the luck I've had not getting knocked up, I should buy a lotto ticket.

Jason slithers up on top of me; each kiss he trails up my stomach to my lips makes me growl louder. Finally, he eases himself in, and a long, low groan of ecstasy comes out my nose. Oooh, not bad, Jason, not bad at all.

"I see you're pretty good with…" I gasp for air. "A fire hose."

He grins, holding my wrists to the floor on either side of my head. Eyes half-closed, I rock with his motions, my breaths ragged. Moaning and gasping, I bite my lip as my toes curl, and reality blurs into a haze of bliss.

"Faster," I gasp.

"I love those little squeaks you make." Jason slows down and lowers his lips to mine.

With a playful snarl, I flip us over and pin his hands to the rug. "I said *faster*."

His eyes widen as I go for broke. For an instant, his expression looks like 'is this where she eats my soul.' Our explosion of bliss is almost simultaneous, though I keep going for a little while longer before collapsing on top of him. His silly grin makes me laugh.

"Still got a soul in there?" I ask.

Jason pats around his chest as if feeling for something. "Think so. Are there such things as succubuses?" He tilts his head. "Succubi? Bae?"

"Who knows? Might be a magical critter out there… or maybe some Shaar'Nath like killing humans after sex like some praying mantis deal."

He brushes a hand over my head, collecting my hair off my face. "You know, I had planned on using the bed… not the floor. Sorry if it's a bit hard."

"Never in my life has a guy apologized for it being hard."

He laughs.

I cuddle up to him, my cheek on his chest, his left nipple an inch from my nose. While I watch him breathe, my brain torments me with what I did to Frank. This man I'm growing more and more fond of… I could rip him apart like a marshmallow peep in the hands of a pissed-off toddler. The idea of that gets me angry with myself. No… I couldn't.

My grip on him tightens. I think I wanna keep this one.

4

PLAYING WITH MATCHES

I woke up late Wednesday and found myself in Jason's bed, with a note informing me he'd gone in for his shift at the firehouse. Crap. It's almost eight. Wow, I haven't slept this late in a while. Guess Jason wasn't the only one who really needed some release. After a lazy shower, I wander around his place for a bit but wind up feeling awkward, like that time I broke into a house for the jollies when I was thirteen. Well, maybe more than jollies. This kid Logan I used to hang out with dared me. Didn't steal anything, nor had I intended to. Roaming Jason's house without him here feels kinda the same, like the owner's going to come back any second and I'll wind up hiding in a closet for hours again until they go to sleep.

There are a couple pictures of—I assume—his mother around, but no one else. Medicine cabinet and fridge have standard bachelor fare, but nothing overly interesting or alarming. I *could* hang out all day, but meh. Using a guy's PlayStation when he's not here crosses some line I'm not sure we've reached yet—a few steps after being comfortable farting around each other, maybe even a step beyond sitting on the throne while he's in the bathroom too.

With the day mostly to myself since he's gone for twelve hours, I decide to head home and do some of that annoying 'adult' shit. I shoot

Jason a text that I gotta do things at home and invite him over after he's off shift. That done, I head out, checking the door to make sure it locked behind me.

Well, now I'm committed. Not getting back in there without smashing something.

Meh. Screw it. Been awhile since I got the thrill of doing something I shouldn't.

I stretch my wings and throw myself into the sky, climbing basically straight up until it feels like people would have a hard time seeing me from the ground. The flight back to my apartment takes a couple minutes, and I land on the roof to be a little more on the subtle side.

My wings evaporate to whorls of black smoke that seep into my back. An eerie sense of someone watching makes me turn and look around. No one is obvious, but I bet it's an Elestari.

"What?" I hold my arms out to the side. "Can't a girl go home?"

No reaction.

A few seconds of silence later, I let my arms drop against my sides and trudge over to the roof access door, avoiding a six-pack of empty beer bottles left behind from whatever happened here last night. The sixth floor is quiet. Hours go by in a blur of annoyances like laundry, sweeping, changing the bed sheets, and cleaning the bathroom. So, yeah, it's a wonderful day off work. Only real good part is trading intermittent cute texts with Jason. Around three in the afternoon, I flop on the sofa and telekinetically levitate a slice of pizza into biting position while starting up the PlayStation.

After I've thrown a few hours into a virtual post-apocalyptic world, Jason shows up at a few minutes to seven with some grocery bags, and goes right to the kitchen.

"What's up?"

"Brought stuff for dinner. Stay put. It'll take a little while," says Jason from out of sight.

Soon, the smell of garlic pulls me away from *Fractured: The Endless Waste*.

He whips up a fairly impressive shrimp scampi over linguine, though we skip the candles. After, we mush together on the couch and play video games for a while until it gets dark, then TV takes over, though neither one of us really pays any attention to the screen. Alas, we both need to report in tomorrow, so we can't stay up too late.

I invite him to spend the night, but we wind up agreeing that if he does, neither one of us will make it to work by six in the morning. So, after a long kiss in the doorway, he heads home and I put myself to bed.

MOST OF THURSDAY DRAGS BY IN A SLOW HAZE OF DRUDGERY. THIS IS good though—it means no one's house is burning down. I make the usual Starbucks run, and cheat a little (telekinesis) to carry twenty-three coffees of various sizes and types the two blocks back to the garage without dropping any.

At 5:39 p.m., the shit hits the fan. The alarm goes off and the station house does an impression of a giant hornet nest some rube just smacked with a stick. Once I'm suited up and on a truck, I spare a few seconds of 'shit, figures…' It's a little irritating that we have a fire twenty minutes before the end of my shift, but it's not as if it would make a difference. This one sounds bad enough that they'd have paged us all anyway. And if I wasn't willing to regard free time as a luxury for when no one's in deep shit, I wouldn't be here. I've got a new frustration these days. Not that I'd accomplish much alone, but I could fly my ass to the fire way faster than the truck will get there. Still, it's not like I'm gonna piss it out all by myself.

The ride to the Elmwood section of Philadelphia takes eleven minutes before the orange glow of fire lights up the street out the windshield. We're not the first department on the scene; the area's already awash with flashing emergency lights and the shouts of other firefighters. It looks a bit like the neighborhood where Jason lives—more row houses—but these are run-down. This section of town is closer in ritziness to where my apartment building sits. That is to say, it's nibbling on the edge of shithole.

Fire has completely engulfed three of the linked houses, and thick smoke billows from the windows of several more in both directions. Crew groups have already formed up in the street, their hoses throwing water into the inferno, but they're not doing much.

When my truck rolls to a stop, I swing out on the door and drop to the street. Shrieking draws my attention to a brown-skinned woman in her later thirties fighting two firefighters and a cop who're trying to hold her back from charging into the inferno. She shouts, "My daughter," and "Santana's in there!" in Spanish again and again until her voice gives way to sobbing.

Time seems to stand still for me. Déjà vu kicks me in the crotch so hard my knees weaken. Eleven years ago, some other firefighter rolling up on a scene stood right where I am now and watched my mother have the exact same meltdown.

The woman points at the leftmost of the three houses in full conflagration. None of the firefighters look willing to go within twenty feet of it, much less inside—too much heat. If Hell existed, this would be it.

"Santana!" screams the woman before breaking into loud wails of anguish.

A faint child's scream comes out of the house.

Oh, fuck being subtle.

I don't even bother going for the air tank/face mask from the storage compartment. As soon as I start running for the door, shouts of, "Amari, stop!" and "Stand down" and "Don't be an idiot" and so on rise up behind me. Humberto even lets go of his hose to grab my arm, while making a 'what the fuck is wrong with you?' face.

"I got it." I shove him hard enough to put him off his feet since he won't let go, and race into a curtain of flames, shifting my eyes to their Shaar'Nath form—glowing pools of dark blue light—to pierce the smoke and blinding glare.

Fire is inherently beautiful to me despite its deadly nature. When my eyes change, the flowing liquid energy becomes more transparent and exponentially prettier. Were no lives at risk, I could stand here and watch it for hours, enjoying the meditative calm.

The roar inside the living room is enough to mute the continued yelling going on from my buddies. All four walls are ablaze. A corridor leads straight ahead past a stairwell against the left wall, heading to a kitchen on the far end of the house. Cinder blocks shatter in the heat and collapse on the right, opening a hole into the next house. Instinct pulls me upstairs. My boots smash half the steps on the way up, sending flaming bits of carpet falling to the basement. Grabbing the wall with my claws stops me from following them. I tear gouges in the drywall and shred the railing as I haul myself to the second story by claws alone. Dedicated as they are, none of the other firefighters hurl themselves in after me. I don't blame them... I have to look suicidal. If I was a normal human, I'd have collapsed from the heat and toxic fumes already and I haven't been in here more than two minutes yet. Their shouting tapers off, but I can't tell if it's because of my focus or if they've stopped. Only the roar of the flames and the distant, horrible wailing of a mother exists to my ears.

Smoke peels off my coat when I reach the upstairs hallway. Three doors belch fire like furnaces, as does the bathroom all the way at the end on my left. There's no chance a kid's alive in this shit. I had to have hallucinated that scream. My heart sinks into my gut; I know what I'm going to find in here, but I will still carry the little body outside to her mother.

I hook a right and hustle past the stairwell, the railing crumbling like stacked matchsticks under my hand, leaving a gaping hole in the hallway. The floor shifts under my weight, sending me staggering into a clawed grip on the wall. I creep onward like a rock climber, heading for a door billowing with flames. Twice, the floor gives out when I step, but my claws hold me up. When I reach the room, I poke my head through a haze of smoke. Another carpet of brilliant orange covers the ceiling. Not-too-distant crashes come from overhead as parts of the roof cave in above me.

The bedroom holds only fire and the fast-disintegrating remains of furniture. It's got the look of an adult's room, so I backtrack. My coat's smoldering, but I don't give a shit. If there's any chance at all I might actually drag this kid out of here, I don't care if the whole world knows what I am. Maybe she did scream and that wasn't a figment of my imagination. Now she's passed out; I've got seconds until she succumbs.

Before I reach the door in the middle of the hallway, a loud *slam* comes from overhead, along with a shrill child's scream from the end of the corridor.

Fuck...

Fire does weird shit sometimes... like leave the ass end of a trailer intact while the rest of it melts. I don't know how that girl's alive, but—some questions you just don't ask.

Rushing as fast as the floor (plus grabbing handfuls of wall) allows, I rush to the last door on the right. The bathroom straight ahead of me no longer has a floor; I think the loud bang came from the toilet falling to the first story.

I'm not entirely ready for the sight waiting for me when I reach the doorway.

At the far corner of a room filled with flames, a shimmering green sphere surrounds a blur of pink. A little girl sits curled up inside a huge hamster ball made out of light beneath a burning section of droopy ceiling that blocks the window six feet to her left. The glass has already exploded from the heat, littering the rug with shards that glint in the firelight.

Of course, as soon as she sees my eyes, she screams.

"Santana?" I shout, darting across the room.

What's left of my heavy fire department coat falls off.

"Don't kill me!" wails the girl.

I catch a flash of terror and... guilt radiating from her. Shit. Did she start this? No wonder she tried to hide. And... how the hell is she still—no. I don't care. She's still alive. That's all that matters.

"Come on, honey. I'm going to get you out," I call in Spanish.

The girl, who's maybe ten, peers up at me from inside her magical shell. She looks untouched by the flame; not a thread of her pink nightie is out of place. A few bits of glass sparkle from her shoulders and hair, and it's in the rug by her feet as well.

"I don't wanna die," wails the girl.

Down on one knee, I reach for her—and my hands pass through the barrier without resistance, into startlingly colder air, like reaching into the freezer for a Hot Pocket. "I'm going to protect you from the fire, okay, sweetie? Don't be scared."

She stares up at me, bawling and trembling. Her guilt intensifies.

This kid is toast if I pull her out of that ball. Not even my former coat would've been enough heat shielding even for a short run… but… oh screw it. Out come my wings.

Santana gawks at me. "Are you going to bring me to hell?"

"Philly's not that bad." I wink and grab hold of her. "Come on. We're just going outside. Your mother is really worried about you. Take a big, deep breath and hold it. Keep your eyes closed."

As soon as she complies, I huddle close and pull her under my wing, using the membrane like a cloak. She clings to my shirt, but stays curled in a ball. Once I'm sure I've got her as covered as I can manage, I stand, back up a few steps, and charge at the burning mass of ceiling blocking the window, driving my shoulder into it. We crash through into clear late afternoon air, and the shouts of firefighters out front become clear again. They've stopped calling my name and are trying to coordinate hoses on the house I went into. The inside of her magic bubble had felt cold to me, but after being in the midst of an inferno, the outside is arctic. When I unfurl my wings, an unexpected jolt of pain paralyzes me for an instant.

Ouch, fuck.

Couple splinters in the membrane.

Jaw clenched, I bite back a scream and hover in place while waiting to adjust to the temperature change. Got a couple splinters in my arm too. They itch like mad while my body forces them out.

Since the row houses have no gaps between them for a quite a distance in both directions—only an alley runs among backyards and small fences—I whirl around and zip upward. Santana gasps for air and holds her breath again, her eyes still closed.

"You can breathe. We're outside," I whisper.

Flying in a wide circle, I glide over the roofs of non-burning houses and come in for a landing behind a crowd of locals gathered to watch the show. As soon as my semi-molten boots hit the ground, I retract my wings. The fire seems to do a good enough job of holding everyone's attention; no one notices me. At least, no terrified screams ring out.

Perhaps lacking in politeness, I shoulder my way past the gawkers and beeline for the sobbing woman sitting on the curb across the street from her former home. Two cops sit with her, one on either side, offering comfort. My throat closes up with a lump at the memory of my mother in the same situation, believing me dead.

The female officer notices me first and gawks. Fortunately, I've got enough of my uniform left that I still appear to be a firefighter. Tears slip out of my eyes as I approach the woman.

"Ma'am? Your daughter's okay," I say in Spanish.

"Mama!" yells Santana.

The woman looks up, blinks, and passes out.

"Mama?" asks the girl.

"Be right back." The male cop jogs to a police car and pops the trunk.

His partner wakes the woman and helps her sit up. She looks up at me, awestruck as I hand the child off. The same way my mother did eleven years ago, she bursts into heaving sobs, clinging to the girl, who gets a distant look in her eyes.

The male cop runs back with a blanket, which he wraps around them, then stands and nods at me. "Nice work."

"Thanks, but I'm not done yet." I smile at the woman and rush back to the fray.

Lieutenant Sims gives me an unhappy look across the hood of his department Tahoe, but doesn't stop me from diving in with the hose crews. Jason runs up and claps me on the shoulder before setting a helmet on my head.

"You okay?" he yells.

"Thanks, and yeah," I shout over the din, while lugging the business end of a hose through the front yard of Santana's house. It's still so hot here, the others haven't dared getting close. "I'm fine."

He falls back a few steps and helps support the hose. The guys start shouting at me about being too close again. No sense doing the total freak show in public. I give some ground and open up the sprayer, still hanging closer than a normal person could tolerate.

It takes us a couple hours to beat back the burn, but we manage to contain the destruction to five residences. While we're wandering among the smoking skeletons of the former houses, throwing water everywhere to make damn sure the fire's quenched, Baker, O'Keefe, and Lancaster call out that they've discovered a body.

"Poor bastard," mumbles Jason.

I stiffen, keeping my hose trained on a stubborn patch of embers in a wall one building to the left. That kid definitely radiated guilt. She probably started the fire, but I don't think she knows someone died. My jaw clenches. Screw it. I'm not a cop. If the fire investigators can't trace a burn back to a kid playing with matches, they don't deserve to catch her.

"Yeah," I whisper. "Lucky there's only one."

"No shit." He looks around and lets out a whistle. "This would'a been a lot worse if it happened late."

What did that kid do? "You got that right."

Once I no longer sense lingering combustion in front of me, I make my way around the wrecked walls. Other firefighters continue policing the area, spraying water wherever smoke shows itself. An inch or so of black muck sloshes under my boots as I head for a place where the cinder block wall separating the row houses has cracked and collapsed, creating a passageway between the individual homes. The body's face down in what had been the kitchen, only a few paces in from the back door.

Hmm. That's bizarre. This guy's six feet from the backyard. Why'd he stay here and burn?

I shift my jaw side to side, again weighing whether or not I should mention anything about that girl possibly having started this fire. She did not feel guilty enough for murder, more like an accident. And it makes no sense this guy burned to death so close to an exit.

Most of this house is gone; only a few timbers hint that a second story once existed. I'm standing in a channel between two cinder block walls full of smoldering sections of roof. This has to be where the fire started: it's the middle of three worst-burned properties, and of those, it's suffered the most damage.

Hmm.

Guess they're leaving the deceased in situ until the ME gets here.

Nah. Fuck it. The fire didn't even start in that kid's house. Not sure what she's guilty about, but I'm not going to mention it. Not my job.

5

SOMETHING MAGICAL

O dd looks come my way the whole time we haul hoses into a stack at the rear of the truck, prepping for the drain and packing routine. The back pats happen too, and a few whispers about magic drift around as well. Obviously, since the Fire Marshal's Office tapped me to 'help with the weird shit,' a rumor's started that I might be a Pyromancer. Or one of the partial mages. Mom referred to herself as a luminare at one point. I think that's what mages call people who have 'a little magic' but aren't strong enough to do the impressive tricks. In Mom's case, her magic's all about divination and well, basically fortunetelling. If she'd been a full mage, she could probably see the future, but she's only got a little gift. And Mom's grateful for even that. She's *way* too nice.

I might run with the 'baby Pyromancer' angle. People would probably take that in stride more than the truth.

Lieutenant Sims approaches me while I'm folding a hose up, giving me a 'need to talk to you' stare along with a 'follow me' wave. I nod at him, but finish the current hose and pack it before walking over to his Tahoe.

It's an instinct out of my control at this point. As soon as I approach, my eyes project the innocent 'I didn't do anything wrong' face that always happens when I'm about to get in trouble. "Sorry about losing another coat."

Sims sets his hands on his hips, shaking his head at the street. "Amari, I don't know whether I should be congratulating you on saving that kid or reading you the riot act for doing something so reckless." He lifts his head to look me in the eye. "And I have no idea how you survived that."

If this had been Lieutenant Pirelli, I'd have asked him if he was disappointed, but I like Sims. "It looked worse from the outside."

"Yet your fire retardant coat burned." He's clearly not buying that idea.

"It wasn't reckless."

Sims raises both eyebrows. "You've got one hell of a messed up idea of reckless. That scene was so hot, we couldn't get within twenty feet of it." He runs a hand up over his hair, clutching the back of his head for a second before his arm drops. "I... what's going on here, Amari?"

He's not looking to make trouble for me. Feels like he's trying to wrap his brain around the unexplainable. And, well, he's been a pretty standup guy to me so far. "Lieutenant... it's a little complicated and I don't fully understand it myself, but what I did wasn't reckless because fire doesn't hurt me."

"Fire doesn't hurt you..." He purses his lips.

"Before you think I'm crazy, I ran into that mess and here I am, not even a first degree burn." I look around at the civilians still watching like this is some kinda damn sporting event, plus all the other fire-fighters. "Can we hop in the truck for a little privacy?"

"Sure."

He walks around the nose to the driver's door, and we get in at the same time. A few seconds pass in uncomfortable silence.

"You know about the fire that happened when I was a kid, right?"

"Yeah. It's why you wanted to join the department." Sims gives me the sympathetic smile.

I do the slow nodding thing. "Yeah. Only, something weird happened that night. I had no way out of my room. It was a fire code nightmare; the window had been bolted shut with an air conditioner. The reason I had no clothes on when I ran outside is my pajamas burned off me while I crawled out. Something magic happened that night. That's why I didn't apply for the investigator position. I wanted to stay on the front line for stuff like *this*." I gesture at the house. "That kid…"

He bows his head. "Yeah. Amazing she made it."

That girl has a few tricks of her own. She's got to be a mage. That green barrier blocked fire but nothing else. Broken glass went right through it, as did my hands. This, I have to bounce off Natalie later, but I keep that part quiet for now. If they learn she's a mage, they'll probably blame her for the fire even if she had nothing to do with it—oh, that's why the kid was radiating guilt. She knows how some people are about mages. No, that'd be fear. Shit. Guilt is guilt. That kid did something.

Sigh.

"Kinda farfetched," mutters Sims.

"Be right back."

I hop out and jog over to McCafferty, who I know smokes. He's still packing hoses into the back of our second truck. "Hey Mike."

He looks back, smiling. "Nice job with that kid. Balls of steel. Guess that burn looked a lot worse than it was."

"Yeah, it did. Wouldn't wanna hang out in there though." I chuckle. "Hey, I need to show Sims something… can I borrow your Zippo?"

"Sure." He hands me a lighter emblazoned with the FD insignia. "Don't lose it though. Belonged to my dad."

I hold it up and make the lid *clink*. "No problem. This'll only take a second."

He nods and goes back to packing hose.

Sims stares at me walking over with an inquisitive head tilt. After I climb in and close the door, I hold up the Zippo. He watches me run the flame over my fingers for a moment, without the slightest change in facial expression or damage to my skin before he waves dismissively. "Fah. Magic. Okay, I believe you. Please stop. That's unnerving as hell."

You know what else is unnerving? Fourteen-foot wingspan, horns, and a tail. I cackle with glee inside my head, but only release a sly smile into the world as I snap the lighter closed.

"Any other tricks, or are you just fire-resistant?" He asks, then shakes his head while chuckling.

"You know, I don't even really need all the gear on."

He gives me a pointed look. "Is that why you wound up naked at the hotel fire?"

"Not by choice." I explain how I blanked out the memory of the fire when I was twelve. "I had no idea I had any special strangeness until the hotel blaze. I got hit with a backdraft that should've killed me. Sorry for fudging the report. An exploding magical device didn't eat my clothes. I stood in fire and survived; the gear didn't."

"Hmm."

"They send girls home from school for showing their shoulders. I'm not planning to start nudist firefighting. I promise I'll be as normal as possible unless something like this happens." Again, I gesture at the building.

Lieutenant Sims taps the storage case in the center console, perhaps a poor attempt at the drum line of a song he's thinking of. "All right. Are you planning to go through an evaluation at the Academy of Magic?"

"Wasn't high on my list of shit to do, no…" I shrug. "I'm no mage."

"Yet, you don't burn." He rubs his temple. "This magic stuff goes way over my head."

"Magical effects are impermanent. A mage casts a spell, and something happens for some set amount of time. I'm psychic, Ell-tee. Remember, that getting visions from touching stuff thing? The whole reason the FMO wanted me on that case? Something like one-hundredth of one percent of the population of mages have psychic abilities too. It's only happened like five times in recorded history. And besides. I didn't 'cast a spell' to make myself fire-resistant… I just am."

"What if it wears off?"

Oh, it won't. I grin to myself. "Well, it's lasted since I've been twelve, so I'm pretty sure it's permanent."

"This is a lot to process. I'm not sure if I should put this in your file or just report that you got incredibly lucky tonight."

I fidget my hands in my lap, staring at them.

"Now, why do you look so guilty?"

"I know you're only the second Lieutenant that I've worked with, but I respect you a lot. There is something more, but like I said, I don't fully understand it… and I don't want to give you more stress. You've already got plenty."

"Ain't that the truth?" He leans back in the seat and lets a sigh out his nose. "How bad is it?"

"Not bad. Just *weird.*"

He glances at me.

"How do you feel about alternate dimensions?"

"I'm gonna bail out here." He smiles. "Nothing dangerous, is it?"

I emit a somber laugh. "Not in the way you're thinking. There's some… people who might try to hurt me, but *I'm* not dangerous."

Lieutenant Sims stares out at the wet, ashy mess of former houses. "It's gonna twist my brain in a knot if you explain this, isn't it?"

"Probably. Kinda an 'upending everything you thought you knew' situation." I smile. "You sure you don't want to hear it?"

"Yep. Positive." He grabs his hat, snugs it on, and opens his door. The chime pings a few times before he turns his head to make eye contact. "Tonight, you heroically saved a child… and got lucky as hell."

I flick the Zippo open and closed. "Understood, sir."

6

THE DOOR'S OPEN

F riday's pretty much a hazy blur. Since I got home late after the fire, I went straight to bed only to wake up a few hours later and do the zombie shuffle back to the station house. Most of the crew has the same idea, and the bunkroom winds up full. After waking again closer to noon, I grab a quick shower. No one who designed this building ever imagined a woman would be a firefighter, so there's one locker room with four shower stalls... but at least they're enclosed. The guys are cool about it, at least outwardly. One or two bristle at the unwritten rule that none of them can shower if I'm in there, but that's cheaper than remodeling the station. I also try to clean up at home whenever possible and avoid using this one since it's such a logistical problem, but after last night...

On the way from the shower to the locker area, a towel covering me from armpit to knee, I wave my Orchid Rain bottle at Herlihy. "Hey dude, you can still borrow the body wash if you want."

Brian's like six-foot-six, probably in the mid-300 pound range, with a bright red barbarian's beard. He's kinda like a higher-level version of Jason... if they were video game characters. He shakes his head, chuckling as I go by.

"Yo, Amari, when are you gonna challenge Herlihy to arm wrestle?" asks Lancaster.

Lamar Burke rubs his arm, looking over with a glint of schadenfreude in his eye.

I put my soap in the locker. "It wouldn't be a fair contest." Once I'm done hiking my panties on under the towel, I turn my back to the room and slip into a sports bra. I don't even own one of those torture devices with the wires.

Herlihy nods at the guys. The set of his jaw tells me he misunderstood my meaning. Oh well, no reason to burst his bubble. Extraplanar heritage *is* technically cheating. No way would a woman my size stand a chance arm wrestling him without something extra going on, and wow am I 'extra.' I give Lamar a telekinetic ass squeeze when Humberto walks behind him. Once the shouting starts, I laugh to myself and finish pulling on my uniform.

The debriefing meeting on the fire is routine, and not as boring as usual. Only one man died, the same one I saw. A handful of other people suffered minor injuries, mostly inflicted by accidents sustained while fleeing the burn. No word yet from the arson investigation unit, but they generally don't burden us with those details. We spend an hour and change going over our response from a tactical standpoint. The general consensus is that the scene had been too far gone to make entry. Lieutenant Sims absolves the room of any guilt in not rushing in there in search of Santana. He calls me out on being brave and reckless, and says that while the end result worked in everyone's favor, I got lucky.

A couple of guys murmur about me scaring the shit out of them. I teeter on the verge of admitting to the whole crew that I can't burn, but Sims redirects the topic to the upcoming charity barbecue we're holding. Once a year, we fire up an enormous cinder block grill along the side of the station house and sell ribs. Half the profits are going to the Children's Hospital of Philadelphia, the rest into our equipment maintenance.

The rest of the day goes to cleaning trucks and gear… and I get another new pair of boots.

Saturday morning, I wake up late and find Ashley curled up at my side with her flying faerie toy. Huh what? I don't remember anything about watching her. Oh hell. She's still got a key. It's around her neck on a metal bead chain. She stirs when I sit up.

"Hi," she whispers. "Mommy had to work. Can I stay with you?"

Ugh. Feed a pigeon once... Of course, as soon as Ashley gives me the cheesy smile, I ruffle her hair and drag myself off to the kitchen to make pancakes. "Yeah, it's okay."

Can't leave the kid alone.

Jason arrives about eleven. Impulse gets the better of me, and we wind up making a day trip to the Philadelphia Zoo. I get a text from Tracy about ten to four saying she'll be leaving work in fifteen minutes and probably home by quarter after. I talk her into meeting us for dinner at this franchise bistro type place. It's hardly pricey. All their food comes out of a rune oven, but it's still decent. Guess they have a properly enchanted one that doesn't screw up now and then, randomly swapping flavor and texture.

Ashley's a flurry of chatter over dinner about the zoo. Her mother's understandably a little glum, since she has neither the time nor the money to take her around like that. Later, when Tracy and I slip off to the bathroom together, I confess I didn't even think of that when the idea to go hit me, and assure her—*again*—that I'm not trying to 'steal her kid' or make her feel like a bad mom. The whole room-mate suggestion slips out, catching her off guard.

"Uhh, wow. Thanks. I, umm..." Leaning on the sink counter, she stares down and kicks at the floor. "That's like, wow. Umm. It's something to consider."

I nod while washing my hands. "Figured it might make it easier for you to do that night school thing." Is it shitty of me to hope she doesn't want to? I mean, the two of them could use the help, but I kinda like my privacy. Guess it wouldn't last forever; only until she gets a better job.

She fusses at her hair, about a quarter inch of brown showing at the roots of her bottle blonde. "I'm still trying to work out how to pull that off. Starting to give serious thought to, umm, *dancing* again."

I shrug. "It's how I got through college. Nothing wrong with it, but you gotta be careful where you go. Some places are pretty scummy."

"Yeah." She gazes into the sink like a fortuneteller. "Thanks for watching Ash so much… and for… you know…" Tracy sniffles and gives in to tears.

I can't really say it's not her fault since she put up with Frank for weeks after the MMA bouts started, but I guess to be fair, she probably didn't suspect what he'd really been after. Then again, maybe she did… it did take quite a while for her to leave Ashley alone with him. Hard to say if she simply feared violence and didn't understand what he wanted to do to her, or if she suspected and took the risk anyway. Desperation totally sucks. I lean close to the mirror and pick at my right eyebrow. "No problem."

Tracy sniffles back her crying into a wet laugh. "Wow, you really turned out to be a friend. Never expected that the way you used to glare at me."

"Wasn't personal. Noise. I have to drag my ass out of bed at five to get to work…"

She cringes. "Sorry."

"Hey, over and done with." I gesture at the door. "We should probably get back out there before Jason sends a search party."

Tracy laughs and spends a moment collecting herself so she doesn't look like she'd been crying. "Okay."

SUNDAY, I'M STUCK WITH THE KID AGAIN. TRACY HAD THE OPENING shift, so Ashley slept over. Her mom was out the door at 5 a.m. to open the Starbucks by six. I'm feeling lazy, sorta kinda my natural state, so I head to Kwan's Market for egg sandwiches. I know the eggs are like from a carton or something, probably fake as hell, but something about them is addictive.

Mr. Kwan stares at me from behind the register the whole time I'm in the store, getting coffee, shadowing Ashley as she picks out a juice, and waiting for some seventeen-year-old part-timer to make our breakfast. His 'am I about to die' expression finally gives way to a smile when I approach the register.

"Morning," says Mr. Kwan. "I should thank you, but I can't explain what happened."

"Ehh." I shrug. "It's dangerous to get between a girl and her donut."

He chuckles nervously and rings us up.

"Bye!" Ashley waves at him with a big grin, and follows me out the door.

We munch on our way to the bus stop. Grr. Yeah. I keep putting off that whole car thing, but it's going to have to happen at some point. After a boring bus ride, we walk a few blocks to Natalie's house. I spend the morning and some of the afternoon on the back porch enjoying the sun with Natalie while Ashley plays in the pool. She doesn't own a swimsuit, but underpants work as a standby. Later, she runs around the yard in one of Natalie's T-shirts while the dryer does its magic.

Is using telekinesis to play Frisbee with a kid while lounging on the porch 'lazy parenting' or genius? Natalie's astounded that I, of all people, wound up looking after a child. I think my mother would be pretty shocked too, but Ashley's nowhere close to the hellion I was—though she did pester Natalie a bit to teach her magic. Speaking of which, I ask Nat about the other kid with the glowing green hamster ball.

"Hmm." Natalie wags her head side to side, thinking. "You know I'm an enchanter, so the strongest effects I can pull off have to be bound to items. Direct 'spells' that work for me aren't the most grandiose things. However, that does kinda sound like an elemental shield."

"It had to be... the condition of that room. Glass fragments went through it, so did my hands. And it was cooler inside. Without that magic..."

"Yeah." Natalie rubs my arm.

I 'catch' the Frisbee and toss it back to Ashley. "Is that a Pyromancer spell?"

"Not necessarily. Destroying or negating is easier than creating. Elemental shields are somewhat universal. I could probably manage one if I studied it enough. Why? You think she might've started the fire?"

"Yeah. She felt guilty about something."

"Oh. Maybe it happened accidentally?" Natalie shrugs. "Some newbie mages can generate sparks when flubbing magic, but something like that wouldn't have started a big fire. Even a kid would've been able to stomp it out before it got too far. Especially if she's a Pyromancer."

"You'd think Pyromancers would work for us, putting crap out." I laugh.

Natalie giggles. "Oh, they're much better at creating than diminishing. Fire is what we call an 'angry' element. They *can* reduce it, but it's maybe five times the effort. If she's new at it, or hasn't been properly trained, she might not even know she *can* 'unmake' fire. But… you still don't even know that she's a mage."

I run both hands up over my head, grabbing handfuls of hair at the back of my neck. "Argh. There's something there but I don't know what. Or if I should even worry about it."

"Ehh… I wouldn't." Natalie pulls her sunglasses down and leans back. "Why does it bother you anyway?"

"Her mother… When we rolled up to the fire, it reminded me so much of when my house burned. That girl's mother was outside freaking just like my mom."

Ashley's run for the Frisbee slows to a walk, and a full stop two steps later. She gazes transfixed at the roof of Natalie's house for a moment before scrunching up her nose at the sunlight and gazing off to the side, as if watching something fly away.

Sigh.

Damn Elestari.

She runs over, bouncing on her toes. "Someone was standing on the house. He had wings! Are they mad at me for summoning you?"

Natalie snickers.

"No, Ash." I poke her in the belly, grinning. "They're nosy."

She nods hard, throwing her hair around. "Yeah. It's not nice to spy on people."

"Right." I squint up at the roof behind me, but it's empty. Hmm. Guess there's something to that 'kids and pets see stuff' thing. Ugh. Being followed by Elestari is only slightly more irritating than having the cops checking up on me every week. "Crap, it's almost two. I gotta get her home."

"Cool. Wanna grab dinner later?" asks Natalie.

"Oh, yeah! I found this awesome Portuguese place." I wave Ashley over, give her a little hug, and a nudge to the door. "Go on inside and get dressed. Time to go home."

She stares longingly at the pool. "I wanna swim some more."

"We can come back. Your mother's going to be home from work soon."

Ashley hangs her head, mutters, "Okay," then trudges up the steps onto the deck, and into the house.

Geez. I'm not doing anything wrong or cruel, but why do I feel like I've just shot her dog?

———

AFTER AN IDLE MONDAY OF 'ME TIME,' IT'S TUESDAY AGAIN. I STAYED UP too late last night on the PlayStation. I tend to forget stuff when I'm overtired. Like clothes. I realize I'm still wearing only panties when a blast of cold air hits me on the way out of my building. The sudden chill wakes me out of my drowsy haze in an instant.

Shit.

Fortunately, my need for keys is variable. My apartment's door has enough of a gap that I can see the locking bar and pull it aside with a telekinetic nudge. I scramble into my clothes and make it to the bus stop with seconds to spare.

Today, I announce the Starbucks run as I am in dire need.

A little past ten, after a few routine hours of no one's shit burning down, I'm squatting on top of an engine that's parked half out the garage repacking hoses when a silver sedan pulls up to the station. Ugh. The car screams 'undercover cop.' I almost laugh. Why do they bother? The guy would be less suspicious in a marked panda car with lights.

The driver hops out, pulls down his sunglasses, and looks over at the building. He's Asian, probably Chinese, with a short buzz cut, a tight shirt, and a wiry, muscular body. He obviously works out, but he's no Conan the Barbarian. A glint of sunlight flashes off his right hip from the detective's badge pinned there as he rounds the front bumper of his car and walks over, Glock tucked under his left arm on a shoulder holster. Something eerily familiar about this guy bugs me, but I can't put my finger on it. He's maybe late twenties or early thirties, but he doesn't have that 'rookie gleam' in his eye. I'd be jealous of the way some people look young for a long time, but I think I got him beat.

O'Keefe is running a broom around the driveway, so he makes first contact. The men mutter briefly before the new arrival's gaze follows a pointing finger straight to me. Deep-seated instinct kicks in and I find myself frozen with that 'oh, shit, what did I do?' paralysis. Crap. This is about the shooting at Kwan's Market, I bet. Okay, calm down. Self-defense.

"Miss Amari?" asks the detective, as he walks up alongside the truck I'm on.

I must look like a frightened teen about to be nailed for criminal mischief. At least for a few seconds until I read his intention... he's not 'after' me. The man wants help. Say what?

He tilts his head, a look of concern in his eyes. "Is something wrong?"

"Umm. No." I manage to keep my voice sounding more or less normal. "Yeah, that's me."

He smiles. "I'm Detective Zheng with the Philadelphia Police, but please, call me Emerson."

"I'd introduce myself, but I guess you already know who I am."

"Yes." He leans against the truck. "Do you have a moment? I'd like to talk to you about something I'm working on."

"All right. One sec." After crawling to the back end, I climb down to the bumper, jump to the floor, then walk around the pumper truck dusting myself off. "What's up?"

He extends a hand, which I confusedly shake. "I was talking to a friend of mine who wound up working on an arson case a little while ago. Your name came up. Word is, you're a psychometrist?"

Oh. *That's* where this is going. Whew. "Apparently. I'm still kinda learning."

"Hoping you could help me out with a case that I'm stuck on. It's not exactly standard procedure, but I'm running out of options."

I squint at him. We're about the same height. This close, I've got a feeling he's a little older than my initial guess, maybe pushing forty. "You look kinda familiar."

Emerson grins. "It's not breaking in if the door's already open."

Whoa. I blink, then laugh. Now I remember him… He picked me up a few times as a beat cop when I'd been in my early teens. The 'not breaking in' line was my weak ass excuse the time we got picked up for B&E after we snuck into an abandoned store at a failed mini mall. Rumors claimed the old department store was haunted, and we wanted to check it out. It wasn't like the place had anything worth stealing, but someone saw us go in and called the cops. He tried the 'long heartfelt talk' to turn me around, which might've worked better if I hadn't been handcuffed to a steel table at the time. "Oh, wow… congrats on the promotion."

"Thanks." He chuckles. "Been a while."

"Yeah it has. You still hate arresting kids?"

Emerson sighs with a nod. "Nothing bugs me more about this job. Sad state the world's in. Kids ought to be all sweet and innocent."

I bite my lip and flare my eyebrows at him. "I can be sweet, but I'm still working on the innocent thing."

A little blush tints his cheeks.

"I'm teasing." Of all the cops that I'd run into over my life, I think this guy stands out as being one of the nicer ones. I never had a *bad* experience like you sometimes see where a cop body-slams some teen into the floor. While I might've occasionally (okay, more than occasionally) let a snide remark slip, I mostly worked the big-eyed innocent face to its utmost advantage. "I'll help if I can. What's up?"

It's his turn to slouch with relief. Great. He's not going to arrest me, and I'm (hopefully) going to make his life easier.

Emerson's expression shifts grim. "There's a serial killer out there targeting the homeless."

"Ugh. What the fuck is wrong with people? Those poor bastards on the street have it bad enough without some shithead hunting them."

"Yeah, but it gets even weirder." Emerson scratches at the side of his head. "The killer is stealing the victims' bodies out of the morgue afterward as well."

Blink. I stare in shock while my brain fumbles trying to understand why someone would do that. "Whoa."

"I've been going in circles trying to find this guy. He's preying on the most vulnerable. People who no one will miss, no one will notice. It's been a giant pain in the ass trying to follow up on any leads. Two morgue workers have also been killed, we think because they caught the guy in the act."

I scowl at the rooftops across the street from the fire station, wondering if any of those sanctimonious 'angels' are watching me now… or if they'd give a shit about someone killing humans at all, much less society's unwanted. "Uhh. No promises, but I can try. I'm still learning my way around this whole 'getting visions' thing."

Emerson nods. "I understand. Anything you can do is going to be more than I've got going for this case."

"Yeah sure, why not." I look back into the garage, but Sims is nowhere to be seen. "I'm off duty at six, or is this an interdepartmental cooperation type deal?"

"I was hoping to borrow you right away." Emerson tucks his sunglasses into a pocket and steps into the garage. "Let me talk to your lieutenant."

"Sure." I point over my shoulder with my thumb. "He's back there."

7

A LITTLE KICK

Lieutenant Sims is cool with me leaving early to help Emerson, on the condition the detective drives me to the scene of any fire we get dispatched to. I'm still technically working for the city in a way. It feels so weird to be helping the police. Really, I never disliked them, at least not in a hatey kinda way. More like how kids grumble at parents for interfering with fun. If I'd developed a genuine malicious streak, my opinion of cops would likely be radically different... and I'd also probably be in real prison now. Sigh. Thanks, Mom.

So yeah. Brooklyn Amari is sitting in a police car again... up front. And it's one of those 'so normal it's obvious' undercover jobs without the cage separating the back seats. We're heading to the morgue in hopes I can get something off the deceased worker or some random object in the room. Since Emerson has nothing at all to go on, he's hoping I can pull a vision out of my ass.

"So, why me?" I raise an eyebrow at him. "Don't the cops have their own psychics?"

He chuckles. "Two, and they're both unavailable. One touched something they shouldn't and has been hiding under his bed for the past few months. Kimberly's drowning in work. I got quoted three months minimum. Guess my case isn't important to the mayor since it's only the homeless being victimized."

"Grr. That's shitty."

"Yeah." He sighs.

"Umm. What did the other guy touch?"

"Some kinda dark altar. Demonic sacrifice or some nonsense like that."

I smirk. Well, it had to be *something* to drive a guy nuts, right? But demons? Oy. Humans will believe anything.

On the ride, I tell him about the crystal, Linzval, and the reading I got from it. As far as I know, it's still sitting in an evidence room somewhere since the police couldn't put together enough to hand off to the district attorney. Rossellini, the restaurant owner, has managed to duck being charged. Meh. Not my problem.

We pull up to the Joseph W. Spelman building, an imposing four-story fortress with these weird windows shaped like upside down Ls. It houses the Medical Examiner's office, as well as the morgue. Security on the way in is pretty significant, which further elevates the oddity of someone stealing a body undetected. How the hell did the killer get in here at all, much less make it out with a corpse? A faint tingle washes over my face as we approach. There's an enchantment in the air here. I bet it's like a detection/security thing.

Oops. I really hope it isn't going crazy after getting a whiff of me.

I'm on edge as we approach the doors, half-expecting a legion of pitchfork-and-torch-carrying rednecks to troop in out of nowhere. 'Course, those idiots would probably try to burn me alive. A sudden laugh from total silence gets Emerson to almost trip on flat ground and stare at me.

"Sorry. Randomly thought of something my friend said last night. Stupid joke."

He shakes his head, probably thinking I'm nuts or something. My history with the cops sure isn't helping that opinion I bet. Once we go inside, he chats with the security staff, a man and a woman, for a few minutes. Eventually, a tall, thin guy with round glasses and fluffy blond hair emerges from the back and approaches us. He looks like the kind of eccentric scientist you'd see in an anime movie who builds an android out of spare parts he scavenges from a junkyard.

"Detective Zheng?" asks the man. "I'm Dr. Roth."

"Yes. Thank you for making time for us." Emerson gestures at me. "This is Brooklyn Amari with the fire department. She's going to be assisting in the investigation."

The doctor nods. "Very well, this way."

He leads us past a card-swipe door into a chilly hallway with a black floor and numerous pairs of steel double-doors. I feel like I've stepped into a level from a zombie video game. Seriously, I tend to have a pretty blasé attitude about scary shit, but something about this place needles under my skin. When Doctor Roth whacks a button on the wall to open a room, I jump.

Emerson looks over at me. "Bad vibes?"

"Nothing but my imagination running away with itself. I play too many horror video games." I exhale hard. Might be a good idea for me to clear my head. "This place is on the creepy side."

The doctor leads us into a room with an exam table, a couple of foreboding counters full of equipment and sharp things, cabinets, and a whole wall of ominous square hatches. I've seen enough cop shows to recognize a body cooler, even though this is the first time I've ever laid eyes on one for real. Subconsciously, I stuff my hands in my pockets so I don't touch something by accident and get an unwanted vision.

Emerson and I stand off to the side as the doctor opens one of the heavy hatch doors. He grasps the end of a sliding tray and pulls it out to reveal a body under a teal sheet. The rattling metal echoes loud; this room has nothing soft to mute sound. Everything about these surroundings is clinical, and as cold as the dead. The tray hits full extension with a sharp *click*, and the doctor uncovers the crushed face of a dark-haired woman who might've been in her thirties. Oof. It's damn near impossible to guess what she looked like in life.

"So, how's this work?" whispers Emerson.

I shrug. "Normally, I have to touch what I'm reading."

The detective starts to give me an uneasy look, but I approach and put a hand on the woman's shoulder. My lack of hesitation makes him squirm. "What? It's a dead person."

He raises one hand in a 'go right ahead' gesture while taking a half-step back. Weird. I'm sure he's seen worse than this in his career, but maybe it's the whole morgue deal that's getting to him.

"Okay, lady, what happened to you?"

Since no vision pummeled me right away, I assume this woman's death didn't involve a lot of strong emotion. That makes me think she didn't see it coming, so didn't have a chance to be terrified. Also likely that the killer didn't regard the act as emotionally significant.

I close my eyes and try to mentally feel around for that little 'energy slice' at the forefront of my brain. When coaxing the vision the second time out of the crystal, it took me a while to get the sense that anything had been imprinted on it. Now that I know somewhat how to look for it, I manage to locate a 'psychic doorway' in about ten seconds.

When I push it open, the darkness of my closed eyes gives way to my flying down a shifting tunnel of light that bursts open to become the same room we're standing in. I'm looking out of the woman's eyes as she's adding drops of something to test tubes of bodily fluids. The *rattle* of a body tray sliding out behind her makes her scream and jump, throwing one of the test tubes randomly to the side. She spins around, butt pressed against the counter. My point of view stares at a single open door in the body cooler, but before she can do anything, a flash of knuckles fills her vision. Pain explodes across my face, and the next thing I know, I'm flat on my back staring up at fluorescent lights while stars dance over me. My cheek feels like I stuck my head out the window of a moving car and smooched a stop sign.

"Ow. Son of a bitch." I grab my face, cradling it.

Emerson takes a knee and puts a hand on my shoulder. "What happened? Are you all right? You fainted."

"Miss?" Doctor Roth also crouches and stabs me in the eye with the beam of a tiny flashlight. "You flung yourself to the floor. Are you experiencing any pain?"

"Only in my face… where that woman was hit." I rub the spot. "It's not real... I think I got a peek at her last few seconds of life. Someone punched her."

Emerson helps me up. "Are you sure you're all right? That looked painful."

"Yeah. Sometimes these visions have a little kick."

"Hmm." The doctor, seeming satisfied by what his penlight tells him, puts it away. "Evelyn's injuries are consistent with blunt force trauma to the face. The pattern of damage does match a human fist, though I believe it was a rather unique weapon."

"A weapon?" asks Emerson. "Not a punch?"

The doctor walks over to a computer and pulls up some X-rays on a giant monitor. "The extent of damage to the facial bones and orbital socket is too extensive in my opinion to have been caused by a fist. I believe your killer may have a medieval fetish. I found reference to a specific kind of ancient weapon, a 'fist mace.' It's basically a metal fist on a stick."

"That's not what I saw, doc." I rub my still-sore cheek. "A dirty hand... unless this guy painted a weapon to look like skin. You're not accounting for magic or... other things."

Doctor Roth shifts his weight from leg to leg, discomfort clear in his expression.

I walk over to the cabinets, pointing at the second door from the left on the lowest row. "This door was open when Evelyn died. Who was in here?"

"One moment." Doctor Roth turns his attention to the computer and types.

"Hmm." Impulse gets the better of me, and I yank the door open before he responds. The chamber has no current occupant, so I pull the tray out a little.

Another vision thrusts itself into my brain within seconds of my hand touching the metal. My surroundings shrink to the narrow confines of a space in the body cooler. There's no sense of fear other than my personal claustrophobia at feeling trapped; irritation permeates this vision as my feet kick at the door... bare feet with a toe tag at the end of hairy, male legs. It doesn't hit me right away how pale they are, considering I'm used to being literally as white as snow, but unless this guy's also half Shaar'Nath, he shouldn't be that color. My sense of confinement shifts to one of agony, like hundreds of icy needles jabbing at every inch of me. No matter how I flinch or twist, I can't get away from them.

A shriek tears out of my throat.

"Brooklyn?" Emerson's shout snaps me out of the vision.

He's come up behind and thrown an arm around me. I'm slumped over the tray, my real legs still kicking the floor while I hold myself up by my arms. The pain's gone… I stare into space for a moment or five adoring that fact.

"You okay? You were groaning and growling." Emerson's right eyebrow is trying to reach the back of his skull.

"Yeah. Another vision." I back away from the body freezer and pace around to give my thoughts a chance to swirl together after being whacked with a mallet. "Whoever was in there didn't want to be in there… and they were in a buttload of pain."

Doctor Roth approaches with a tablet. "The last occupant of that drawer was a Mr. Charles Nelson." He sighs. "Poor bastard… Few things bug me about our country as much as the way we treat our veterans. Absolutely shameful leaving them to the streets."

Emerson sets his hands on his hips and shakes his head, eyes downcast. "This guy was one of the victims from the case I'm working on. I'm sure my suspect killed this woman in the process of stealing Mr. Nelson's remains."

"Are you sure?" I point at the hatch. "The man on that slab wasn't dead. I saw him kicking at the door trying to get out."

Much of the color in Emerson's cheeks fades. "Umm. If he was in there, he would've been dead. Any chance that vision of yours is subject to interpretation?"

"You saw me reenacting it… kinda. Are any of this guy's victims still in custody? Or have all the bodies been stolen?"

Emerson sighs. "All nine. Though if you're right in saying Mr. Nelson wasn't dead…"

"Maybe there's a new drug or something out there that makes people *appear* dead until it wears off?"

Doctor Roth swipes his finger at the tablet screen a few times. "Toxicology reports on Mr. Nelson found alcohol, marijuana, and trace amounts of OxyContin."

"Was an autopsy performed?" asks Emerson.

"No. I hadn't gotten to him yet. I only had the technicians processing bloodwork and conducting a preliminary external visual examination." Roth shrugs. "I suppose it's possible the man might not have been dead yet, but I cannot explain how numerous police personnel as well as my initial field exam of the remains concluded him deceased. If there *is* some new illicit drug out there, in my opinion, it's extremely dangerous. That man appeared so close to death, I'd lay fair odds many of its users don't 'come back.' However, we didn't find any traces of an unexplained chemical in his system."

Emerson sucks on his teeth, giving me a hopeful stare. "That's what I'm hoping Miss Amari can answer."

"I can only do so much, but I'm trying." I look around the room. "Is this gonna be good for one of those 'don't give me a ticket' cards?"

He chuckles.

"Hmm. Nothing really stands out. Doctor, do you still have the phial Evelyn chucked across the room?"

"No, I'm afraid not." He crosses his arms over the tablet, held tight to his chest. "It was incinerated with the other biomedical waste late last night."

Damn. That might've been useful. "So it looks like someone must've known this guy wasn't dead and came back for him. But... why kill Evelyn?"

"No witnesses," says Emerson. "Funny thing is, the video surveillance didn't catch anyone entering or leaving."

I try placing my hand on Evelyn's shoulder again and focusing, but I only get the same 'wonderful' close up of knuckles again. The second time, I'm ready for it, and the vision doesn't put me on my ass. "Looks like an actual fist, not a weapon. Her attacker was standing off to the side. She didn't get a look at him."

Doctor Roth grimaces. "It would be exceedingly unlikely. At least, not without the person breaking most of the bones in their hand." He covers Evelyn and slides her back into the cooler.

"Who says they didn't?" I shrug.

"Also," says Doctor Roth, "the extent of the damage is quite severe. I can't imagine a person having that much power in their fist except for perhaps a professional fighter at the peak of their training."

I can imagine it. My punch put a golem on its ass. Fair bet if I slugged a person as hard as I could while fully shifted, I'd probably mash open their face as bad as this poor woman's… or worse. I'm not in any hurry to test that. Nor do I say anything about it. Poor Vince Milligan. No wonder I cracked his pelvis when I kicked him in the balls. Oh well. I didn't know back then, and the little bastard did punch me in the nose. "Let me poke around a bit and see if I get a read on anything else in here."

Emerson gestures at the room. "Go right ahead."

8

CHAUFFEUR

As soon as the car passes, I leap out of the bushes and sprint across the street. Jose, Gina, Aiden, and Logan break cover and follow. The rhythmless clap of our sneakers on parking lot feels like the loudest sound in the world. Giddy with the thrill of adventure, I lead the charge toward the supposedly haunted old department store and flatten myself against the wall in a shadow spot. It's chilly tonight, and even with my denim jacket, I can't stop shivering.

My friends all think I'm scared, since none of them are 'that cold.' Logan's convinced the building's packed with ghosts, and he's already shaking as much as I am... only I'm not scared at all. This is fun as hell. Can't blame him too much, he's the runt of the group... still thirteen.

I creep past a 'no trespassing' sign and pull a board away from the barricade they put up to block the entrance. It comes off in my hands with barely any effort. Wow, guess they really aren't trying that hard to keep people out of here.

The others form a single file line behind me, with Gina close enough to hump me. She's still seeing space goats from all the weed we hammered this afternoon, but the girl has no tolerance whatsoever. I'm clear as shit already; it kinda sucks. That crap wasn't cheap.

"Lynn... you think it's true?" whispers Jose.

I shrug and stick a leg in the hole I made. "No clue. That's what we're going in to find out."

"We might find Sam Smith," says Aiden. "You think he's still in there?"

"Dude." Jose rolls his eyes. "That's a bullshit story. There ain't no kid named Sam Smith."

I slither past the barrier and stand up in a small space between it and a pair of aluminum-and-glass doors, dusting splinters off my black jeans. "There *was* a Sam Smith, but he couldn't have disappeared in here. "He went missing in 1981. This strip mall wasn't even here then."

"Didn't last long," says Jose with a laugh as he crawls in. "What was this place anyway?"

"Fail is what it was." I squint up at the blank façade over the entrance. A hint of old lettering on the wall looks something like 'Strohman's.' A single mannequin looms in the window, a male torso and head with no arms on a post. "Some kinda department store."

"What happened to it?" asks Logan while crawling in behind me.

I stroll up to the doors. "Probably Amazon."

Sure enough, they're locked.

"Aww, shit. Game over." Gina yanks on the doors, shaking them before she sways to the side, watching something glide by that isn't there.

I frown back at her. Who wears a hot pink miniskirt to sneak into a place at night? Black leggings and T-shirt—good. Pink skirt? Ugh. Might as well wear those sneakers with blinking lights in them and wonder why you can't lose the cops.

"Hey, Lynn." Jose sidles up behind me. "Wanna mess around later?"

I lean up to the glass in the door, trying to get a view of the inside while he rubs my ass. "Maybe. Mom's working late tonight so we could use my room."

"Cool," mutters Jose.

"I hear them." Gina walks straight into the door. "Ow."

Aiden and Logan laugh.

"Hey Gonzalez, you sure you didn't get Khadafy Weed?" Logan snaps his fingers at her face.

"Huh what?" asks Gina.

Jose snickers. "She's way too high for straight up pot. That shit had to have LSD in it too."

"Stuff didn't hit Brooklyn at all," says Logan.

"Yah, but Lynn's a pro," says Jose.

"Didn't feel like anything unusual." I shrug. "High didn't even last that long." I scoot to my right, trying to get a view of the inside latch. Oh, there it is. Little deadbolt nub. A telekinetic tweak makes it turn, and the door unlocks with a *click*. "We're in."

I pull the door open with showy flourish, doing the butler bow.

Once the guys file in, I ease the door closed behind us. On the off chance there's actually some kinda haunt in here and we need to run in a hurry, I leave it unlocked. A nasty smell like wet sneakers hangs in the air, probably coming from patches of dark mold staining the drop ceiling tiles overhead.

"Whoa, this place is creepy." Logan advances off to the left, weaving among empty round racks full of clothes hangers.

"Yeah." Jose's bravado fades from his voice.

Gina heads straight ahead along a white linoleum pathway that used to run between the different display sections. Most of the room's been cleared out, leaving it a massive open space. The occasional piece of shelving or freestanding clothes rack remains. Metal cables hang from the ceiling here and there with electrical wiring poking out the ends. Patches of floor glitter with the shimmer of smashed fluorescent lights. Maybe a hundred yards away, a pair of dead escalators have become a stairwell to the second floor. Some interior walls deeper in still appear to be intact, one still labeled 'housewares' in large white letters.

"You feel anything?" Aiden's voice quivers.

"Nope." I shake my head and wander at random into a cashier's station inside a U-shaped counter, where I pick among a bunch of drawers and cabinets. The electronics are long gone. I told these guys I can move shit with my mind, so they think that lets me see/feel ghosts for some reason. "Is it in yet?"

"Ooh," mutters Jose. "Cold."

"Huh?" Aiden looks over at us with a clueless expression.

Oh, he's adorable. A fourteen-year-old who's as innocent as a sixth grader. Should I fix that?

I take back what I said. Logan's not the most scared, Aiden is. He's the 'good kid' of the group, who only started hanging out with us a couple weeks ago, since we were the first ones to talk to him. He just moved here over the summer. Who moves *to* Pennsylvania anyway? There's nothing to do here but drink, have sex, and go to the gun range… and I'm too young to buy a gun. 'Course, I'm too young to drink too, but I don't let that stop me. The cops are a little softer on that than they'd be on me running around with a firearm, though. Not that I really want one. Drinking is fun. Guns, not so much.

So that leaves me two out of three.

Hmm. Do I want Renee pissed at me? 'Officially,' she and Jose are dating now, but she's been avoiding him. Or at least always seems to be busy. Hey, I don't mind being the revenge girl as long as he's at least halfway decent. He's gotta be, right? He's two years older than me at seventeen. Not sure where people get their information from, but I've only *done it* twice. So what if it happened with two different boys?

Eh. I'll figure out how I feel about that later.

Aiden's afraid of getting in trouble. Not like we intended to pressure him into coming along, but Jose's 'it's cool, you don't have to go' sounded unintentionally like a dare, so here Aiden is.

"Have you been dead long?" asks Gina.

Abandoning my fruitless search of the cabinets, I pop up over the counter and peer at Gina. She's nose-to-nose with a mannequin.

"That's a dummy, dumbass," says Logan.

"Oh." Gina sidesteps it and heads for the escalators.

We spend about twenty minutes roaming around the downstairs with our flashlights before heading up the escalators into the former furniture section. Two queen-sized beds remain along with a shitload of drywall panels. Looks like whoever got hired to clear this place out took an extra-strength dose of Fukitol and walked before they finished.

"Hey ghosts," calls Jose. "You guys real?"

Aiden spins around with a gasp, like he heard something. "What was that?"

"A ghost!" hisses Logan, after sneaking up behind him.

"Aah!" Aiden jumps and almost falls over. "Jerk! Don't do that."

Jerk? Really? Oh, he is too innocent.

Broken bits of wall and other crap crunch under my boots. We fan out, exploring the much smaller upstairs area. The place had an in-store food counter, and it's kinda fun to roam around the kitchen and check out the massive refrigerators. It would be better if they had something in them other than a stale smell.

"Hey, where's Gina?" asks Aiden.

"Asleep on that bed downstairs." I randomly gesture at the wall, no idea if I'm even pointing in the right direction. "She's stoned."

"Guess she ain't got your tolerance," says Jose.

"Guess not." I check my pockets and find one joint. Ooh, cool. Thought I was out. I saunter over toward Jose, holding it up between two fingers. "Maybe this'll help us see a ghost or two."

"Right on," he says.

I step on something that shoots out from under my boot and sends me stumbling forward. The joint sails into the sink. Jose stands there stunned, watching me fall flat on my face.

"Whoa." He helps me up. "You couldn't do that again if you wanted to. Shit went *straight* into the drain like a fuckin' bullseye."

I half climb into the sink, shining my flashlight down the pipe. If I can see it, I can pull it back out with telekinesis. "Where'd it go?" Shit! It's gone. "Grr! Fuck!" I yell. "I hate my luck!"

"Aww, it's just a joint." Jose pulls me close, smiling. "You can get high on me instead."

"Oh, really." I grin and grab his crotch. "Think you'll last longer than that weed?"

I hop up to sit on the counter with Jose standing in front of me.

We spend a while kissing and making out. His hand goes up my shirt, so I stuff mine down the front of his pants. Right as we're seconds away from abandoning care and going all the way right there on the countertop, Gina screams.

"Shit," I gasp.

Jose kisses the crook of my neck, making me shiver. "Later?"

"Yeah. Guess we gotta watch the kids."

He laughs.

After fixing my shirt and putting my jacket back on, we hurry out the kitchen door to find Aiden shaking and whimpering like a six-year-old who'd just had a nightmare. Whoa, that scream didn't come from Gina. It takes all my self-control not to laugh at him as I jog over.

"What happened?"

He points. "A... a shadow moved by the wall. Looked like a dude walked outta the kitchen."

Jose shakes his head. "No way man. Nothin' in there but us."

Out of the corner of my eye, I spot Logan creeping up behind Aiden. Biting my lip, I wander off to the right. Seconds later, Logan leaps and grabs Aiden while emitting a meaningless shout. For a second or two, I'm not the palest person here. I *almost* get worried that he's going to pass out, but Aiden starts breathing again.

Logan laughs. "Got you!"

"Yeah." Aiden takes a deep breath and lets it out slow. "You did. This place is freaky." He trots after me. "Brooklyn... I swear I saw, like a shadow man, over there by the wall."

"Yeah huh. There's nothing there, and nothing out here."

We find a few mannequins in the swimwear area, which when all we've got are flashlights, is pretty damn unsettling—even without ghosts. There's something about not-quite-human shapes standing perfectly still that picks at the back of our souls and puts us on edge.

However, it offers the perfect opportunity. I make one wobble with telekinesis, close enough to Logan that he hears it. He stops walking with a gasp, and swivels his flashlight around. The beam flickers over a skinny female mannequin as he pans right. A quick nudge rotates it, and when he pans back, he stops with the beam focused on it. The light spot wobbles.

"Uhh, guys…" Logan points. "I think one of the mannequins is moving. I swear it was facing the other way a sec ago."

Aiden, halfway across the room, freezes and gulps.

Jose chuckles. "Dude, leave him alone. You got him bad enough already."

"Naw, man." Logan shakes his head. "Not messin' this time."

"Your head's playing tricks on you," I say. "There's no ghosts in here."

Logan keeps his beam on that mannequin for a little while more before he resumes walking around.

"You didn't say there's no such thing," says Aiden in a weak voice.

"Oh, ghosts are real." My grin turns wicked. "I don't see any in here though… but… hang on. I think I feel something. Some kind of energy."

Everyone stops moving and looks toward me.

I strike a dramatic pose with two fingers of my left hand touched to my temple. "There's a restless energy…"

"In Jose's pants," mutters Logan.

Almost laughed. Damn, that was good. Managing to keep a straight face, I make a show of turning in a full circle as if 'sniffing' the air. "I think it's over by Logan."

He gasps. "Where?"

The instant he raises his flashlight, I telekinetically grab the mannequin and send it sliding straight at him.

Logan lets off a shriek that sounds like a preschooler. He darts off at full speed and nearly falls down the escalator. The mannequin crashes into a display rack and drags it to the floor, making Aiden and Jose both yelp in alarm.

I'm done. I hit the floor laughing my ass off.

Jose catches on first and chuckles.

A low whimpery cry comes from downstairs, like a little boy who'd skinned his knee. Aww shit. Guess I scared him *too* much. Still grinning—it feels wrong to laugh out loud at a kid who's sobbing for his mother—I head for the deepest part of the upstairs, what looks to have been the part where they kept the good shit: TVs, stereos, and video games. Though, when this place closed down, there might not have been home systems… or they had like real primitive shit.

Jose and Aiden go downstairs, muttering about checking on Logan since he's crying like a little kid. Well, he technically *is*. Thirteen is still a kid, right? I'm like mature and shit at fifteen.

I make it only a few yards deeper into the room before a dark apparition coalesces in the middle of the linoleum pathway. It's obviously a man, though I can't make out any details. Strangely enough, as freaky as it looks, I'm not scared of him at all. Normally, I can read the intention of people, so what they look like doesn't matter. This thing… no read at all. But something about him radiates non-threat.

After a moment of staring at him, I raise a hand. "Hi. Did you, uhh, die here?"

The silhouette shakes its head and points.

"What? You died out there?"

I swear it makes an annoyed grunt. The same kind I often make when trying to explain schoolwork to Brittany Cortez. The girl's a total airhead. Wait… a ghost just called me stupid.

Before I can narrow my eyes, he points at me again, and I catch a brief glimpse of myself plunging through the floor and landing on a whole bunch of sharp, pointy shit in the basement—after breaking through the ground floor. I blink and take a step back. The figure's gone.

"Whoa." My heart thumps in my chest. I'm alone on the upstairs floor and I just saw a *real* ghost. And he warned me… Right. Time to go home.

As if the floor is ready to crumble out from under me at any minute, I tiptoe back to the escalator-turned-staircase. From the top, I have a good enough view to spot Logan sitting on the foot end of the bed. Gina's got her arm around him. He's still sniffling and shaking, though Jose and Aiden look like they're struggling not to laugh.

I rush down the stairs and head over to them.

"Dude pissed himself," says Jose.

"Not funny." Logan mumbles, red-faced. "You didn't see that ghost."

"You guys want the good news, the bad news, or the weird news first?" I ask.

All of them turn to stare at me. Gina doesn't look quite as messed up now. Guess those power nap things actually work.

"Umm, weird first," says Gina in a hazy voice. She's a little bleary-eyed, but doesn't sound totally stoned.

I point up. "I saw a real ghost. Aiden's right. Black shadow man."

Aiden once again gets close to matching my paleness.

"What's the bad news?" asks Jose.

"This building's gonna collapse. I almost fell through the floor."

Logan sniffles and stands, revealing that his jeans have gone dark down the front. Oops. "We should get outta here."

"Yeah," says Aiden. "What's the good news?"

I walk over and stand by Logan, folding my arms. "Nothing tried to hurt you. That was me."

He blinks and stares up at me. "What?"

I point at a fallen ceiling tile and levitate it. "Just fuckin' with you."

Logan slugs me in the shoulder. He looks pissed, but doesn't hit hard at all. "Bitch."

"Heh." I wink at him.

Aiden shoots me a quick grin of thanks when no one's looking at him.

"Come on... let's go," I say.

I lead the way out the door, cross the gap between the entrance and the barrier, and duck to crawl through the hole. When I stand back up, my heart just about stops. Two police cars are pointed at me, along with four guns. Jose bumps into my calves.

"Dude, why'd you stop?" mutters Jose.

It takes a second or five for my muscles to unlock. I swallow hard, shift my weight onto my knees, and ease my hands up. "Uhh..."

"Easy," mutters one of the cops to his buddies. "Just a bunch of kids." He stares at me and nods to the side. "All right. Over there."

I walk to my left as indicated. Somewhat relaxed, the officers lower their weapons.

Jose crawls out, looks up, and mutters, "Shit."

Logan drags himself out next and freezes. He eyes the parking lot.

"Don't run," I say. "They hate it when you make them chase you."

Two of the cops chuckle.

"Listen to your friend," says one. "She knows the drill."

"Hello, Miss Amari," says a deep voice.

I summon my most innocent expression. "Hi, Officer Pruitt."

Oh… holy shit! I am *so* lucky that joint went down the sink. If I had that on me…

Aiden bursts into tears as soon as he sees the cops. He drags himself out, continuously mumbling, "Sorry" as he stands petrified like a deer facing an oncoming truck. Gina falls flat when she emerges, and doesn't bother getting up.

"Guys, I'ma sleep a bit, 'kay?"

"Cops, Gina," says Jose.

She lifts her head up and waves at them. "Oh. Hi."

The cops put their weapons away and walk over. A Chinese guy who looks on the new side strolls up in front of me. "What are you kids doing?"

I glance at his nametag. "Officer Zheng… we were looking for ghosts. Everyone at school keeps saying this place is like super haunted… so we wanted to check it out."

"Breaking into a condemned building?" He asks.

My grin exudes cheese. "It's not breaking in if the door's open, right?"

Officer Zheng laughs, but forces himself back to 'stoic cop' in a few seconds. "You realize this is private property. You're all trespassing."

"She cuts so much school, she can't read the signs," says Gina.

"I do not!" I glance sideways at her. "I'm *late* a lot." Ooh. Zheng's radiating concern. Awesome. The big eyes worked. "Ever since I was like nine, I gotta drag myself outta bed and make my own breakfast 'cause my mom's sleeping. She works real late."

Jose knows I'm trying to play the sympathy card, and holds back the sigh.

"Come on, you lot." Officer Pruitt waves us over to the car. "Hands on the car, spread your legs apart."

Aiden keeps crying, begging them not to tell his parents, but trudges over.

As soon as Zheng starts patting me down, I mutter, "Careful with Logan. He pissed himself."

The boy glares at me. "Shut up."

"She's just trying to score brownie points," says Gina.

I shift as the cop checks my pockets, holding still. At my age, it's still pretty unlikely a cop will grab something they shouldn't, but hey, if it'd let me off with a warning, whatever. "I see these guys so much, we have a working relationship. I'm just being courteous. Would *you* want to get a handful of someone else's piss?"

The cops chuckle. Logan still gets patted down, but the officer doing it puts on blue latex gloves first. We luck out in that none of the others have any contraband, or at least any that the cops find. Zheng handcuffs me to Gina, my right wrist to her left, and puts us in a car. The boys get similar treatment and are loaded into the other car.

Grr. Guess I don't have to decide if I'm doing anything with Jose tonight.

Zheng hops in the passenger seat with Pruitt behind the wheel. The older white dude is muscle-huge and bald, and the whole car rocks as it absorbs his weight.

"Are we in trouble?" asks Gina.

"We'll see." Zheng looks through the grating back at us. "Guy across the street saw flashlights inside and called it in."

"Doesn't look like you kids did any damage or stole anything," says Pruitt.

"There's nothing in there *to* steal," I say. "But we did see a ghost."

"Once we get to the station, we'll call your parents and sort everything out." Zheng pauses to give me a reassuring look before facing forward.

Pruitt makes eye contact with me via the rearview mirror, chuckles, and starts driving. "I think I'm in the wrong uniform. I'm basically this kid's chauffeur."

"The limo's looking a little rough, and the wet bar is empty." I fidget at the cuff. Can't help it. I *hate* them. "Mom's stuck at work 'til like two in the morning. Maybe you could just like take me home and come back tomorrow afternoon to talk to her?"

"Nice try, kid." Pruitt grins. "Your usual suite is waiting."

Shit. I let my head fall back against the seat.

9

ACCELERANT

The juvenile holding cell isn't what most people think of when the word 'jail' gets mentioned. My reserved suite at the Casa de Law is a small room with beige-painted cinderblock walls, an ass-busting cot, tiny toilet/sink thing, and a plain steel door. No bars. No one can see me inside, except for whoever's watching the screens at the other end of the camera in the ceiling behind the bulletproof glass.

My first stay happened when I was eleven. It scared the shit out of me more than anything else has, though it didn't have any real effect on my continuing to do bad stuff. Even at fifteen, seeing the cell picks at the mental scab, reawakening my initial fear from the first night I'd been stuck here and slept in 'not my bed.' The worst part was that no one told me anything about what would happen to me. I had no idea that night if I'd ever go home or see my mother again.

As it turned out, I'd been 'out too late' for my age and held on a curfew law that they rarely enforce. Because my mom worked the graveyard shift at the diner and didn't own a cell phone, they couldn't find her. While they sorted out who I belonged to, my narrow ass sat in a cell, trying like hell to cry in silence.

By now though, juvie's not a big deal. Feels like I'm renting a room for the night. Okay, I'm still a little scared, but the cops here are pretty cool. As much of a pain in the ass as I can be to my mother, I never give the police (much) attitude. Since I'd been in and out of the station so often since something like eight, everyone knows me. It helps that I don't do really *bad* things too. Sneaking into the store tonight had been probably the legally worst thing, though I'm not sure how breaking into an (ostensibly unlocked) abandoned property stacks up against vandalism.

Oh well. I asked them to let Mom know if she's too tired, she can pick me up in the morning. As much as I'd rather sleep in my own bed, I can cope with this if she's beat. I know how that diner kicks her ass. The cops don't expect to hold me long. I can tell because they let me keep my clothes and didn't make me put on one of the brown jumpsuits.

I bet some detective is poking around inside the place now to see if we broke anything. Seriously, how is causing damage to a building that's gonna get torn down a crime?

A few minutes after I stretch out on the sad excuse for a bed, an irritating beeping/buzzing noise starts up. The featureless walls offer no clue about its source, and I can't think of what else it could be. It grows louder and more insistent. Argh! What the hell! This is cruel. I hop out of bed and lift the mattress, but the plain metal shelf has nothing that could be responsible for the noise. After pacing the cell for a moment, I start pounding on the door.

"Hey, something's making noise in here. Can you guys please stop it?"

Usually, they come to check on me in a minute or two, but this time, I'm ignored.

"Hey!" I pound on the door. "Someone? What's this damn beeping?"

It gets even louder, like my brain is vibrating with each ping.

Argh! I grab the sides of my head and slide to sit on the floor, my back against the door, fingers in my ears. It doesn't help much. The maddening buzzing tone doesn't let up.

Beep. Beep. Beep.

I glare at the toilet. The damn noise is *so* annoying, the idea of mashing my head into the wall to knock myself out starts to feel like a good one. This alarm clock from hell is—

Shit.

I'm dreaming.

The juvie holding cell disappears as my eyes open. I'm curled up on my bed with my fingers in my ears, my real alarm clock losing its little goddamned mind. Best use for telekinesis ever. Snooze button from fifteen feet.

Ahh. Blessed silence.

I roll flat on my back and stare at the ceiling. Damn. Vivid-ass dream. Had to be from talking with Zheng on the ride home after the morgue. An hour and a half of roaming around touching random things hadn't given me anything useful. Zheng floated the idea of a temporary strength boost from magic, but the doctor still thought whoever punched Evelyn would've broken their entire hand.

Oh well. I did what I could.

Since I've overslept by thirty-five minutes, I rush a shower and skip food. Screw it. I pull on a racerback shirt, my uniform pants, and boots. If I rely on public transportation, even without breakfast, I'm going to be late. My polo in hand, I run out and go to the roof.

Jumping off makes me laugh at the memory of the first time I did so, when I cruised straight into the wall of a building down the street. I've gotten quite a bit better at flying these days. My wings unfurl with a leathery ruffle and carry me up into the sky. PEPTA buses can't compete with a couple hundred miles an hour as the crow flies. Two minutes later, I swoop in for a landing behind the Starbucks I walk to from work.

"What the fuck was that?" says a man in the alley nearby.

Oops.

My wings collapse to wisps of black vaporous energy that seep into my back. I duck around the other corner while pulling my polo shirt on, evading the man coming the other way. Like nothing at all abnormal happened, I stroll inside and grab a venti black coffee plus an egg sandwich. A young guy with dark skin walks around the building looking confused. He enters, glancing around, but doesn't bat an eye at me. Whew. He didn't get a good enough look.

Crap. I need to be more careful about flying. 'Course, it was an emergency.

I get to the station house with ten minutes to spare. Looks like it's going to be a slow day. Nothing on the schedule. All the maintenance tasks are checked off and the trucks couldn't be cleaner. So, I head to the ready room and hop on one of the general-purpose computers. Time to start looking at that whole driver's license thing. Okay, there are two tests, one paper, one practical. A notice mentions no operator's license is required for enchanted self-driving vehicles, but those things wouldn't dare skip red lights if I have to. Yay for fire department blue lights.

Eventually.

After downloading a manual, I email it to my phone and flop on the couch reading.

Joe Hilleman walks in a little after 9 a.m., and approaches with an expression like a kid preparing to ask for a raise in his allowance.

"Sure." I stand. "What's up?"

"Sure?" he asks.

"You're about to ask me to help with another case, right?" I tilt my head.

He grins. "How'd you know?"

I tap my head. "Psychic, remember? Really... it was all over your face."

"Oh."

"You remember that row house fire last Thursday?"

My thoughts leap to that poor little girl hiding inside a green bubble. "Yeah. I don't think I'm going to forget that one. Something odd involved?"

"Yeah. There's some strangeness to it. Would you mind accompanying me back to the site to look around?" He nods toward the door. "Already ran it by Sims."

I click my phone off and slide it into the belt holder. "Lead the way."

We head downstairs and out to the SUV with Fire Marshal's Office insignia. Once we pull out into traffic, I glance over at him.

"So, how's Lawrence doing?"

"Good." Hilleman smiles. "He's home now, resting. Be out for a couple weeks yet. Honestly, I think he's more upset all that work the two of you did isn't going to help any convictions."

I frown. "Yeah. Sucks." The Mob burning down a restaurant bothers me way less than what that mage Eaves had his dick in. That *had* to be an Elestari he'd been conspiring with. I don't care if the Mob burns down fifty restaurants (as long as no one's in them at the time). Trying to end the world, *that's* an actual problem. I can't tell Hilleman Eaves became a fine red mist, but I think Lawrence should know. Maybe a visit is in order soon.

My phone tweeps. It's a message from Tracy Harper asking if I can watch Ashley. Damn.

I text back: ‹I'm at work. Umm. Natalie might be willing to help. I can ask if you want.›

I'd offer to ask Mom, who I know would *definitely* be cool watching Ash, but she's in Allentown and I doubt Tracy wants to pay for a PEPTA portal.

She replies with 'plz!!!'

I shoot Nat a text. She's willing, even offers to pick her up. Ash is going to love that car.

After sending Tracy ‹Natalie's otw›, I put my phone away.

"Busy?" asks Hilleman.

For the rest of the ride to the fire scene, he gets the explanation of my next-door neighbor having child-sitting issues. Again, I leave Frank out entirely. He nods along with me, and winds up adding some grumbles about people who think food stamp recipients are a waste when a 'government-issue hammer' costs $900.

Hilleman pulls over by the blackened remains of the row houses. The scene's quiet, devoid of spectators. Two cops sit in their patrol car sipping coffee. As long as this remains an active investigation, the police will be here.

As I open the door and slide down to the sidewalk, the internal argument returns. If the evidence trail points at that child, do I want to help throw some little kid into the system? My answer comes back as a maybe. Depends on what happened and why she did it. If she's a little psycho, yeah, better to get her help.

"So, we established the origin point in this house." He points at the most severely burned one in the middle of the devastation.

I chuckle. "I figured that out the first night. All these buildings have the same basic construction, and it's the center of the damage."

"True, but the cinder block walls between the sections aren't guaranteed to fail at the same rate." He strides across the dead lawn. "But, here they did."

We crunch inside after ducking the police tape.

Joe points to the walls in the corridor leading from the living room to the kitchen in the back of the house. "We found evidence of accelerants, but can't explain what on Earth it is."

"Hmm." My gaze follows his finger to a swath of green sprayed on the wall. "This stuff?"

"Yeah."

I lean closer. The substance looks like watered down green paint, but it's not totally opaque. It's also radiating a weird energy. "This is messed up." Whatever this stuff is, it's been sprayed all over the walls, floor, even the ceiling. "Feels like I'm in a slasher video game where they turned the blood green to make it kid-friendly."

Hilleman chuckles.

Following it leads me into the kitchen, to a large stain of the same green stuff on the floor… right where the body had been.

"Doesn't it strike you as significant that there's a giant puddle of it right where the man died?"

"Yep. We figure whatever that substance is, it's the accelerant. We're pretty sure the dead guy was the arsonist who wound up getting trapped in his own blaze. The fire started in here."

I spin around to face him, eyebrow up. "Joe…" My hand goes up, thumb pointing over my shoulder at the former kitchen door. "He dropped dead six steps from the way out. How do you figure he got trapped?"

Hilleman purses his lips. "It's a working theory. Ehh... that's kinda why you're here. I agree it's weak. And we've never seen this goop before."

"Well, let's see if I can do my magic." I crouch by the giant puddle, take a breath, and touch my fingertips to it.

It takes me a minute or two to find an imprint. When I mentally pry at it, a nasty pain jabs me in the chest like I've been run through with a fencing rapier. My body goes limp, but Hilleman catches me before I collapse to the filthy floor. Wheezing and gasping for breath, I can't make my arms obey. A hot sensation, like blood running down my chest follows, and cold tingles creep all over me like an army of ice spiders swarming.

"Gah!" I yell. "Ngh."

Out! Away! Stop! Snarling, I wrench my mind back from the vision. The pain in my chest shifts from agony to a dull ache. Hilleman holds me up until I manage to get my arms and legs taking orders again.

"Holy shit... Ouch."

He crouches eye to eye with me, a look of worry on his face.

"I'm all right. Just a vision." I gasp a few breaths and stand. "This is a lot more complicated than you're thinking it is."

He keeps holding my arms. "Are you all right?"

"Yeah." I rub my sternum. "Wow." So that's what it feels like to get shot as a human. When that punk got me in the arm, it was... annoying. "This guy died of a gunshot wound right in the heart."

Finally sure I won't fall over if he lets go, Hilleman pulls out his phone. "The ME report didn't mention anything about a bullet wound."

"Oh, he definitely got shot. Or had a length of rebar jammed through his heart. I felt it... and his life going away, his arms and legs going numb, the body shutting down." I shudder. "I can't tell if he died here or elsewhere and someone dumped his body in this house, but if he was dead at the time the fire started, it makes sense why he didn't run right out the door. Death kinda has a negative effect on one's foot speed."

"Heh." Hilleman's face glows white from the screen glare. He pages through something on his phone. "The ME doesn't note any injuries on the deceased aside from severe burns and charring over 100% of the body. They had to identify him from dental records."

I tilt my head. "Who was it... and that could still fit someone stashing a dead guy here and making it look like he's an arsonist who got caught in his blaze."

"Umm." Hilleman flips back a few pages. "Deceased's name was Charles Nelson. NKA."

"NKA?"

"Sorry." He smiles. "No known address."

"Wait..." I blink and swivel to face him. "Nelson?"

Hilleman nods.

"Whoa." I point at him. "That's fucked up."

"I'm not quite following. Gonna need a bit more information."

Still staring at the spray of goo, I pace around. "A couple days ago, a dead man named Charles Nelson was brought in to the medical examiner's office, but the body was stolen before an autopsy could be performed." I explain my trip there with Detective Zheng. "What I saw there makes me think Nelson wasn't really dead. But... if this is the same guy, he had to be. That was a fatal wound. I'm sure of it."

"Hmm." Hilleman rubs his chin. "I'll need to talk to that detective."

"Good idea." I point at the floor. "Honestly, I think my friend Natalie should take a look at this green slime. It *feels* strange to me. And if the lab can't identify it... gotta be magic."

Hilleman rolls his eyes. "Oh for f—" He sighs. "Always the damn mages."

I stare at the green puddle. It looks a whole lot like the bloodstain that belongs under a dead guy who's been shot in the heart. How on Earth was that kid involved in *this* mess? Or was she? Where did that guilt come from? Grr.

"All right. Be back in a moment. I've got some sample kits in the truck." Hilleman walks out.

While waiting for him to return, I wander, picking up and examining a few metal objects that survived the fire, but none have a significant mental imprint. Eventually, I wind up poking my head out the back door and looking around the yard.

There's a break in the fence to the left big enough to walk through into the next yard, but no obvious cause. The inward direction of the damage suggests something came from the house next door and smashed the fence toward where I'm standing. I step out and twist to peer up at the roof. It's possible a section of house could've fallen and crushed it. Neither the slats (which are wood) nor the ground in the area of the busted fence look the least bit charred. I step past the breach into the neighbor's yard and spot a long blackened line in the grass that looks like a roof timber or something fell there and burned.

Hmm.

When I turn to go back, a spot of green catches my eye on the fence by the hole. The same substance from inside the house. "Hey Joe," I yell.

He emerges from the back door of the 'fire origin house.' "Amari? Where'd you go?"

"Right here."

Hilleman crunches over some debris in the other yard and trots up to the breach in the fence, peering at me. "What'cha got?"

I point out the green stuff on the fence. "I think our arsonist came in from here, and got some of that mystery substance on the wood. Bet he had Mr. Nelson's remains doused in it already. 'Course that would mean this fence had been broken before the fire."

"This is reaching new levels of strange." He reaches for the spot, but pulls his hand back. "We were treating this as an informational investigation, believing the arsonist already dead... but what you're saying makes it sound more like an open criminal case. We'll need to get the crime scene team in here."

"Good plan. Let me get a sample of that stuff for Natalie first before you seal it off?"

He hands me a phial. "Knock yourself out."

"Already did." I hurry into the kitchen and scrape some of the green gunk from what's left of the floor.

When I hold the vial up, the goo catches the sunlight and glows green. "Well, Mr. Nelson. If you did kill Evelyn, how did you wind up here?"

"Ready?" asks Hilleman.

"Yeah." I pocket the phial and take one last look around the kitchen. Someone sprayed that stuff everywhere. It makes me think of a guy running around with a bottle of lighter fluid dashing it on the walls before striking a match. But, magic users don't need accelerants to burn places down.

None of this makes any sense. A person couldn't mash down a fence, but a normal person also couldn't crush a skull with one punch.

Ugh. This investigation is going to suck.

10

DECEIT

Hilleman drops me off back at the station house since it's not even noon yet. It's still quiet, so I head to my locker to stash the phial for now. When I pull it out of my pocket, the oddest feeling comes over me from holding it, like I'm touching blood. It reminds me of how it felt when I tracked Eaves. I think about Dad teaching me to use it to find someone. Last time I checked, blood is not green. Okay, goblins don't count. Even if I've taken the train straight to what-the-fuckistan, there's not much point following a dead guy. I think he's still in the morgue this time.

One thing I *am* sure of: magic is somehow involved. Santana, that kid I saved, had a spell guarding her. Why was she guilty? Maybe the killer saw her and felt sorry, so he protected her and she's guilty for not telling anyone she saw him? It's understandable she's so rattled, she's refusing to talk; seeing one's entire bedroom covered in flames is pure nightmare fuel. That poor girl's going to have a rough few years.

I leave the phial in my locker and go on about my routine at the firehouse. It's fortunately quiet, which has the irritating side effect of making the day take forever. I'm off the hook at 6 p.m., having read over the driver's license stuff twice. I'll probably read it a couple more times and then schedule the test. I can't ask Natalie to let me practice with her car since that little thing is bonkers. I'm convinced what she does with the steering wheel has no actual bearing at all on where the thing chooses to go.

I behave myself and catch a bus home, calling Natalie on the way.

"Yo," Nat says.

"Hey... I need your help again with an official type thing. Any chance you could stop over?"

"Uhh, sure. I need to bring munchkin back anyway."

I blink. "Ashley's *still* there?"

"Yeah. Her mom never called. Guess she's pulling a double or something. We'll be there in a bit. You eat dinner yet?"

"No."

"Okay, cool. I'll grab on the way."

"Awesome."

Once we hang up, I text Tracy with ‹U ok?›

I get a reply a minute later with ‹Sry! Stuck @ work. Sent txt to ur friend›

Oh, that explains it. Natalie's got an Augur, the magic equivalent of a smartphone. It's basically a slab of crystal with a bunch of magic stuffed in it. Some of them have fancy cases too. Tech companies went utterly batshit about licensing. It's such a stupid rivalry issue, but those things can't get text messages from normal phones. None of the apps are cross-platform too. If you ask me, the tech guys are just pissed off that the Augur's supported full three-dimensional projection with games for years now, and the tech guys still haven't figured out how to do it.

‹Nat's got an Augur. No texts. NP. Ash otw to my place.›

‹UR grape› She corrects to 'great' a second later.

The bus stops at my corner soon after, and I walk the block and a half to my building, make my way up to the sixth floor, and stagger into my apartment. After stashing the phial on the coffee table, I change into a knee-length sleep shirt. Within seconds of me walking back out of my bedroom, someone knocks.

Wow, that was fast.

I jog over and open the door. "Hey Nat—"

A too-handsome-to-be-true blond man flashes me a million-dollar smile. His dark suit looks like it costs more than I earn in a year, but it's probably an illusion. I fold my arms and smirk.

"Hello, Brooklyn. Might I have a moment of your time?"

"I guess. At least you knocked instead of appearing inside my place." I back up and let him walk in, giving the door a light shove once he's past. "You guys might want to dial back the perfection a bit. Now that I realize you exist, it's pretty damn easy to spot you."

He makes this conceited little laugh like I said something cute. "It's all right. I am not trying to conceal my nature from you. I have come to bring you important information, certain facts that should've been presented to you much earlier than now."

This guy gives me sympathy for short girls. I'm pretty much average in that regard, but his chin is over my head. "All right. I'm listening. I already told your friend Graf that I have no intention of breaking anything. Whatever you think you believe about me, the Armistice is my home too, and I like it here."

The man's smile goes patronizing. "Of course. You are destined to save the world."

"Of course I am," I say, deadpan. Grr. Something's oddly familiar about him.

"The demons long ago placed three cursed pillars that are responsible for all pain, suffering, and evil."

"Right." I tap my foot. "Lying is evil, isn't it? One of those 'sin' things?"

"What are you talking about, child?" asks the Elestari.

"Well, for one thing, you called the Shaar'Nath 'demons.' They're not. No more than your kind are 'angels.'"

A twitch in his perfect smile at the word 'angel' tickles me inside. As much as he's trying to sell me a bridge, it appears to be true what Dad said about them hating that word. I guess when you consider humans to be ants, and those ants come up with a pet name for you, it's insulting.

"So you *have* done some research." He nods. "Well, regardless of what you've discovered, you must know that your very existence is the key to preventing the destruction of light and virtue. You, and you alone, will be responsible for ushering in a new age of peace and enlightenment."

I've heard *this* before.

"I grew up believing that my mother had been raped. When I finally met my father, he explained quite a few things that made the rest of my life start making sense. I'd be more inclined to trust the Elestari if you hadn't threatened to kill me when I was a child if my father dared contact me. What kind of monsters are willing to murder an innocent?"

"You spoke to him?" The man's smile fades to a look of alarm. Both his perfect golden eyebrows go up. "He was not to make contact… not to—"

"Corrupt me?" I roll my eyes. "He told me all about that. You kept a father away from his daughter for—" I stare at him. That night in the old department store… the shadowy figure. Dad… *He* must've taken the joint and thrown it down the pipe knowing the cops would've nailed me for it. Wow… he really was with me. "I'm not inclined to trust people who'd be willing to kill a child."

"Of course, your father would say something so vile." He sighs. "Our kind are not subject to the same base urges as the Shaar'Nath. Harming the innocent is anathema to us."

"Except, to you, a half-demon isn't considered innocent. Nor are humans, right? They're somewhere between ants and mold."

He chases a lock of hair away from his face with two fingers. "The humans have come quite a bit further than anyone anticipated. I do not know why your father ignored you for so long, but it's easy to understand why he would lie to you. He should not have made contact."

"Dad said as soon as I realized that I wasn't totally human, he was free to make himself known. You guys gave him an escape clause. Guess you expected by the time I'd gotten old enough to figure things out, my mother would've molded me into an anti-demon or something."

The man purses his lips, glancing out the window. "You discovered your nature earlier than we had anticipated."

"Yeah well... I wasn't going to leave a man to burn to death. Shit happened."

The Elestari smiles, offering me a hand. "There is much you need to learn still if you are going to protect the world."

"Now I know why your voice seems familiar."

He tilts his head in curiosity.

"You're the guy Eaves was talking to. The version of 'saving the world' you're talking about is *your* world. Elestari world, or whatever the heck you call it. You want to destroy this one."

The man sighs. "As you no doubt overheard, we are willing to set aside a place for humans. They are not our concern. The cursed pillars, which by the way are responsible for all human suffering, must be torn down. I will see to it personally that humanity is preserved, but in a way that no longer functions as a wall the evil can hide behind and fester."

I rub a finger across my lips for a moment before pointing it at him. "I'm kinda thinkin' you're full of shit. The Shaar'Nath aren't what you're saying they are, just like not all Elestari are what Dad told me they are."

"Hmph." He shakes his head. "Of time, we have an abundance. Your doubts shall ebb, and you shall eventually come to accept the wisdom of what must be done. I can sense your mother's noble influence has shaped your soul. When the time comes, you will do what is right."

Fists on my hips, I lean at him, eyes narrowed. "And what if what's right isn't the same as what you want?"

"Oh, child. You are young yet. Wisdom takes time." He glances at my coffee table. "Best of luck with your nazedeh problem."

"Wait, my what?"

He fades away into thin air.

Grr. He can't just drop a funny word at me and disappear. Crap! I haul ass to my bedroom and grab my phone to type 'nazaduh' before I forget it.

Hmm. Pretty sure I murdered the spelling, but maybe Natalie will recognize it.

11

THE PILLARS OF CREATION

How do you take the kind of asshole you want to slap the shit out of and make them into the kind of asshole you want to eviscerate? Add wings and a god complex. Grr. I know lies (I ought to, considering how many I've told in my life) and that guy radiated perfect sunshine so strong, a skin cancer screening is probably not a bad idea.

My brain jams to a halt. Can Shaar'Nath or whatever I technically am even get that?

Ehh… I wander over to the kitchen and knock on the table twice. No sense jinxing myself.

"Insufferable," says Dad.

His voice is soft enough that he doesn't completely scare the crap out of me. I startle rather than going statue. Dad's appeared by the front door, shaking his head while clucking his tongue.

"Yeah," I mumble. "That sounded like total bullshit."

Dad slips his hands into his pockets and strolls over. Gah! I hate that my brain keeps considering him sexy… for a guy in his late forties. He hasn't been part of my life long enough to 'feel' like my father, so my eyes and my brain are having a catfight. "Something's bothering you."

"Well. Yeah." I scowl at the door. "I'm over eighteen now. Something tells me the cops won't let me slide for destroying the world because I can make cute eyes."

He laughs.

"That cursed pillar thing is bullshit, isn't it?" I lean my ass against the counter, arms folded. "What was all that about anyway? They're trying to set me up for something."

"You are correct." A hint of pride shows in my father's smile. "Melisandre was trying to trick you into destroying the Pillars of Creation."

My eyes narrow. "Wait, so there *are* pillars? Meli-what?"

"Yes. And that particular sanctimonious pile of golden light was Melisandre. He's more or less in charge of the pack of Elestari who are itching to reignite the war." Dad moves to lean against the counter next to me, and spends a moment tugging at the cuffs of his blazer. "They are the three places where the old magic holds the mortal world intact. They're not literal pillars in the sense of stone columns. One exists in the mortal realm, one in Imbreleth, which is our realm—"

"And one in the land of asshats."

Dad grins. "The asshats call it Aesinor."

Hah! Hearing a man who looks and sounds like my father say 'asshats' with such seriousness is pure gold. "And these 'angels' want me to break these pillars so the Armistice collapses. Meaning, Earth goes bye-bye." I shoot him a playful grin. "How do I know you're not lying to me now?"

His grin fades to an earnest but confident look. "You don't. Trust your instincts... and it's more than merely the Earth. This entire plane would cease to be. Other planets, galaxies as you know them... everything within this dimension."

Whoa. That's hard to comprehend. "Umm."

He bows his head, chuckling. "I imagine you're having some difficulty processing the scale."

"A bit. These creatures want me to flush the entire universe down the drain so they can go back to clubbing each other over the head? What possible sense does that make?"

"My dear daughter…" Dad looks up with an amused expression. "Once those in power have convinced themselves of their own moral superiority, whenever throughout the course of history have they ever held themselves accountable to logic or common sense?"

I laugh. "Are you talking about Elestari or humans?"

He offers a blasé half-shrug. "The only difference is the wings."

"And the lifespan."

Dad glances at me. "Have you seen your government lately? They all seem to be centenarians."

"Heh, yeah."

"Be on your guard." Dad puts a hand on my shoulder and stares into my eyes. "These Elestari will attempt to deceive you, as will some of our kind. Individuals on both sides long for war, though I believe they are still in the minority."

I scowl at the ceiling. "Why me…?"

Dad gives me a squeeze and lets his arm drop. "The Elestari tried this once before in the other direction."

"Other direction?" I quirk an eyebrow at him.

"Yes… in that case, a half-Elestari named Joan of Arc."

"Who?" I scratch my head.

He chuckles. "Slept through history?"

"Depends on the year. Freshman/sophomore, probably. Junior/senior, I was probably baked."

"Baked? But heat doesn't bother you."

I stare at him. "You're mocking me."

"You are my daughter." He beams with pride. "They thought they would have the best chance by playing upon the humans' belief in their mythological 'god' and running with that whole 'angel' thing, even though they loathe the word. As you can imagine, it did not take much effort for a male Elestari to find a human woman who they felt embodied the necessary ideals. They had a daughter, whom they proceeded to groom to believe the forces of divinity spoke to her."

"Oh… I bet she got to have her father around." I kick at the floor. Dad starts to look down, but stops when I take his hand. "I don't blame you."

"Yes… she did. Only, things didn't quite work out in the way the Elestari had planned." He laughs. "In order to reach the Pillar on this plane, one needs to make use of magic. Joan, as well as her mortal parent, developed the unfortunate belief that magic equated to sin, so it became impossible for her to do what the warmongering Elestari wanted."

Even with a hand over my mouth, I can't stop laughing. Tears fill my eyes, and I wind up clinging to my father to keep from falling over until the giggle fit stops. "That's hilarious!"

"Ironic indeed." Dad smiles with more than a little bit of smugness.

"So, is she still around? I mean… thousands of years, right?"

Dad shakes his head. "No. They burned her at the stake."

"They?" I blink. "The Elestari?"

"No… the humans who were too afraid she actually *did* see angels and might contradict their invented religion."

"Oh. That sucks." I look over at him. "Why didn't she like break the post and fly away?"

He shakes his head. "She had not yet discovered her true nature, and still thought herself human. Last I heard, she's still rattling around Aesinor. At least her Elestari side is, and quite pissed off."

"For being burned at the stake?" I raise both eyebrows.

"No… she believed the whole religion thing. Didn't take learning the truth well. One moment, she's 'God's chosen' and the next, merely a pawn between two warring groups." He cackles. "She's upset she's not a *real* angel."

"Geez." I examine my fingernails. "Guess I better keep my mouth shut so I don't wind up burned at the stake."

The serious look I give Dad lasts all of three seconds before we both crack up laughing.

"So, I guess I'm the 'let's try making someone who isn't such a prig' option?"

"Seems so. That is why they forced me to stay away."

I put an arm around him. "That's proof they know they're full of shit."

"How so?"

"If they really believed the Shaar'Nath are as 'evil' as they say, why would threatening your daughter make you do anything?"

He pulls me close. "Your mother did an amazing job."

"Yeah. Would it start a war if I killed the Elestari who told you they'd hurt me a few times?"

"A few times?" He laughs.

"Well, you know. Kill them in the Armistice, they just go back home."

"It would escalate, I'm sure."

Grr. "Oh, Dad? Did you... that time we broke into the old store. Warn me about the floor?"

"Perhaps." He twiddles his thumbs, too innocent.

"Thanks for getting rid of the joint... but you coulda warned me about the cops waiting for us outside."

Dad glances at my door. "Your friend's almost here. And the front door was the safest way out. If the police got out of hand, I would've stepped in."

"What, like mind-wanked them? Did you do anything else for me I never noticed?"

"Little things here and there... like standing outside a trailer to absorb an explosion."

I gawk at him. He saved me... "Wait a sec. I can't burn."

"No, you can't." Dad winks. "But you *were* rather fond of that video thing you stole." His smile fades to a serious look. "And, at the time, I had no idea how much of our traits you'd inherit. Mixing with humans has unpredictable results. I did not wish to take the chance that you wouldn't be immune to fire."

Choked up, all I can do is hug him. His chest is warm like a heat stone. But, before I can pull myself together enough to get another word out, he disappears.

Ooh. I have *got* to learn how he does that!

12

WORSE THAN FIRE

D ad's announcement lets my mischievous side off the leash. Cell phone out and recording, I hurry over to the door and yank it open. Natalie jumps with a yelp, almost dropping an armload of white bags. Ashley goes stiff and wide-eyed, but doesn't make a sound. Giggling, I hit stop on the video and back up so they can walk in.

Natalie playfully narrows her eyes at me. "You're so lucky I don't hit you with a tickle jinx."

Eep. She got me with that once in school. Shiver. "You wouldn't..."

"Hi!" Ashley zooms in, hugs me, and heads for the kitchen.

"Don't startle enchanters. Especially when they're carrying food!" Natalie hurries over to the kitchen table, leaving an aroma trail of Italian food.

"Ooh." I jog after her.

She unpacks a chicken parmesan entree, a baked ziti dinner, and one order of spaghetti and meatballs... plus a large tossed salad. We pot-luck it, each taking a bit of everything... but I think she overdid it. We could've fed another three people with this much food. Ashley chatters excitedly about her time playing at the store, and asks what I did at work. I leave it at telling her I'm trying to figure out who started a fire that ruined some people's homes.

The doorbell rings only a few minutes into our eating. I spin around in my seat and open the door with telekinesis, intent on shouting 'go away' at whoever's bothering me, but it's Tracy.

"Oh, hey." I wave. "C'mon in. You eat yet?"

She eyes the door. "Umm. The door just opened itself?"

"Magic," chimes Natalie.

Tracy's carrying a couple Starbucks bags, I bet a bunch of unsold food they normally throw out. Well, that's something. She sets them in my fridge and joins us at the table. We hang out for a little while after, the three of us in the kitchen bullshitting while Ashley monopolizes the PlayStation. Tracy grumbles that her boss is giving her a problem with her possible night school schedule, since she'd have to leave there at seven three times a week. Natalie suggests doing one of those online classes with no set schedule. Our conversation drifts around normal crap for a good hour or so before Tracy thanks us profusely for the food and watching the kid. Looking exhausted, she collects Ashley and heads home.

We stare at the door for a while in silence once they're gone.

"That poor kid." Natalie sighs. "Let me know if you need any help with her again. She's so sweet."

I raise an eyebrow. "She set up candles and tried to summon a demon. Not sure if she intended to kill that asshole, but... uhh. Kid's got a little dark streak."

"So do we all. If we're pushed enough. So... what's up?"

"Got a sample of some weird stuff I found at a fire scene." I grab the phial and bring it over to her. "What do you think this is? I'm no mage, and even I can feel *something* on it."

"Hmm." She holds it up to the light, peering at it. "What do you know already about it?"

I explain the way it looked sprayed around, and how a big pool of it had collected under the body. "FMO thinks it might be the accelerant, poured all over the corpse. Their theory is the man who died in the fire had been the arsonist. I'm thinking he was already dead."

"It's giving me a sense like blood," says Natalie.

"Yeah. I got that too."

She blinks at me. "You did?"

I tell her about Dad teaching me to use blood to find people. "I got the same sensation that I could use it to follow someone… but if it *is* blood, that dude is quite dead."

"Can I take this back to the shop and do some tests?"

"Knock yourself out." I smile.

"Cool." She drops it in her nauseatingly pink handbag.

"Don't tell me you've got a princess wand in that thing?"

Natalie pouts.

"You do?"

She pouts harder. Before my jaw's all the way open, she cracks up laughing. "I'm not *that* bad. So I like pink and frilly stuff. Who cares? Ooh! You should've seen this unicorn I made for this family."

"You made a unicorn?" I shake my head in disbelief.

"No. Not a real one. A toy." She holds her hands about three feet apart. "Thing is yea big, shoots sparkles from the tip of its horn and stuff. It walks around and can follow simple voice commands."

Sounds cute. And that cute probably cost some rich bastard like eight grand. Sigh. I can't blame Natalie for that, but who in their right damn mind spends cash like that on a thing the kid will forget exists in a year? Bah. Okay, I'm bitter. Whatever.

We eventually wind up on the sofa for a movie. Natalie finds this weird foreign vampire film that's shitty and eerie and engaging all at the same time. Shitty in the sense of production quality, that is. The story's not bad.

Ashley's scream comes through the wall.

"Whoa." Natalie jumps.

As soon as the girl starts wailing for her mother, I relax. "Nightmares. Frank."

"Aww." Natalie frowns. "Kids handle being scared in weird ways. My cousin Esteban almost got hit by a car when he was five. It missed him by inches. He went mute for a few weeks, but I don't even think he remembers it now."

Speaking of mute… My thoughts drift back to that girl, Santana, clinging to her mother after I carried her out of that blaze. She hadn't said a damn word after saying 'Mama!' when I handed her over. With the amount of fear wafting off that kid, she'd seen *something* worse than fire.

"Something spooked the shit out of that girl. More than the flames."

"Huh?" asks Natalie.

I tell her about Santana, the green bubble, and how she'd been way shell-shocked. "She also gave off guilt. If she caused the fire, she would've been able to get away. Why hide in the house? And the fire started one building to the right."

"I'm no psychologist, but it *could* be the fire. She at least knew not to leave that shield spell. Or maybe she saw something that scared her more than burning." Natalie stands and gestures toward the bathroom. "Be right back."

Hmm. That's a good point. I suppose I could try and talk to the kid. I've got no legal authority there, but there's always the hope her family's willing to talk to the woman who saved the kid's life.

13

SMASH AND BURN

The infernal one-note alarm drags me out of sleep. I resist my usual urge to smash the poor, defenseless clock, and trudge to the shower. Today's breakfast is a yogurt/granola cup. While I'm scraping the last bits of purple off the bottom—in the right circumstances, I might inflict serious injuries on a person who tried to take something blueberry flavored away from me—an idea comes down from on high. Or up from below, I guess. If I'm going to make a mythological reference, I suppose I should at least keep the teams straight.

For no particular reason, I let my horns out and bop around the table while head-banging to my imaginary music and making metal signs. Okay, right. The idea. I grab the phone and call my boss.

"Sims," says the Lieutenant.

"Hi Ell-tee. It's Amari. Question. Would it be okay if I took a few hours to follow up on something for the FMO? Hilleman brought me in on a weird case, that row house fire from last week. If there's an alarm, I'll come running." Or flying.

"All right. How long do you think it'll take? What's it entail?" asks Sims.

"I'm hoping to follow up with a witness." No point being secretive, really. I explain the green goop and my need to check with witnesses to see if anyone saw something paranormal.

"Didn't the FMO already do that?"

I smile. "Yeah, I think so... but they might be more willing to open up to one of their own. *¿Tú entiendes?* Probably not more than two hours. If I need more, I'll call and check. If it's faster, I'll just come in."

"Okay. Call me if anything changes."

"Will do. Thanks."

Now for the awkward conversation—Detective Emerson Zheng. I've never called the police before at all, much less a specific cop. I know I'm twenty-three now and also a city employee, but some part of me still can't shake thinking of them as trouble.

"Brooklyn?" Zheng picks up after eight rings. "Good morning."

"Hi, Emerson. I was hoping you might be able to give me some information. The Fire Marshal's Office pulled me in to an arson investigation that I think is related to your case." I lean/sit on the arm of the sofa and tell him about finding Mr. Nelson's body at the fire scene, plus the green spooge all over the place. "And I think that girl might've seen something that could break both cases. Problem is, I have no idea where she is. Is there any chance you can find out and tell me?"

"Hmm. Hang on." A few minutes of silence later, the phone erupts in a cacophony of clattering as he picks it back up. "Looks like they're staying with the mother's parents." He gives me an address in Point Breeze, on Greenwich Street. "Need me to meet you there?"

"It might be better if I go alone. Police might spook her." Especially if she's guilty about something. "Is Mr. Nelson still in the morgue this time?"

Emerson chuckles. "Yeah. Not much to go on. The body was burned too badly to locate any cause of death. ME's taking his sweet time on it."

"He probably suspects Mr. Nelson was already dead when he caught fire."

"How did you know that?" asks Emerson.

I laugh. "I'm psychic. No, really... But aside from that, Nelson was on the floor a couple steps away from the kitchen door. No way he started a fire and got trapped in it unless he happened to suffer a massive heart attack as soon as he lit the match. He could've escaped easily."

"True. All right. Let me know if the girl's any help."

"Definitely. Thanks."

"Oh. If the family doesn't want to talk to you, don't press it? I technically shouldn't have given you that address."

"Yeah, sure. No problem. I'll behave myself."

What? I mean it. I will.

Hmm.

Dad managed to keep all my neighbors from noticing Frank splattered around the alley. I hurry to my bedroom and swap my sports bra for a racerback, and leave my polo shirt off. Time for experimentation. Instead of going out the street level door, I head to the roof. Once I'm at the edge, I close my eyes and concentrate on the idea of not being seen. Okay people. Look the other way. Don't notice me. I'm not really here.

The squidgy little wad of energy that danced around in my head the first time I tried to get my wings to come out happens again. A little focused intent causes it to rise up to the top of my head and expand before tingling away. Hmm. Well I did *something*. Wonder what?

One way to find out.

My wings unfurl to their full span, and I let gravity pull me forward over the side. Philly's got plenty of distractions to keep people's attention on the ground. As long as I avoid the city center and high-rises, I might be safe with short hops… and there's always magic as an excuse. Weirder things than girls with wings have happened in this city. Okay, you've heard of 'blink goats,' right? Normal-looking goats, but if they get startled, they randomly teleport a short distance? Well, we had a blink whale go through town a year or so ago. And since, well, whales aren't supposed to be out of the water, the poor thing remained in a perpetual state of panic for some time. Pretty sure the damage went into the millions.

Catching an updraft, I soar into the clear blue sky of a day too perfect to be worrying about how almost a whole section of row houses burned to the ground or a homeless veteran wound up dead at the middle of it all. This is a beach day. Too bad I'm not a beach type girl. Now, a slammin' concert outside? I'm all about that.

I trade texts with Jason on the way. Nothing overly exciting, but he's trying super hard to be cute. Hmm. Is it illegal to text while flying? Hah. Probably not going to be until a significant number of demihumans die because of it.

My flight takes only a few minutes before I circle over Greenwich Street about sixty feet up, waiting for this dude in a T-shirt and jean shorts on his porch to move. Three minutes later, my patience is gone and I veer off looking for another spot to come down. The end of the block has no obvious spectators, so I glide in for a landing, drawing my wings back in when I'm still a few feet off the ground. After putting my fire department polo shirt back on, I walk along looking at house numbers until I find the Rios home. When I pass Mr. Pain-in-the-ass porch sitter, I can't help myself and telekinetically knock his beer into his lap. He recovers it before *too* much spills, and begins looking around while muttering about ghosts.

Hah.

I approach the house next door to Porch Man and push the button. A fiftyish woman responds to the doorbell, appearing both surprised, confused, and suspicious.

"Hello," I say in Spanish, before introducing myself. "I understand if this is not a good time, but I believe Santana might've seen something important. Can I maybe talk to her for a few minutes?"

The woman relaxes somewhat, but she's still throwing off distrust like mad. Her intention reads as one of protectiveness without hostility, so if the kid *is* responsible for the fire, she hasn't admitted it to her family. "My granddaughter is not well. She hasn't been right since the fire."

"Maybe I can talk to her and help? My home burned when I was twelve. I know what she's going through."

"Mama," says a woman. "Ay! That's the one who saved her." The girl's mother runs up to the door, practically grabbing my arm and dragging me in. "Come in. Please."

"Mary, be careful," says the grandmother.

Mary Rios dissolves into a crying, hugging cloud of rapid-fire 'thank yous' between repeating to her mother that I'm the firefighter who ran in to get Santana out. The grandmom seems like the suspicious type. Maybe I should've gone with the 'just here to see how she's doing' plan?

"Oh, thank you for visiting." Mary hugs me again before stepping back and wiping her eyes. "I don't know what I would've done if you hadn't been there."

"I'm just glad I was." I tell her about my home burning, but go back to the version where I can't remember how I escaped. "My mother thought I'd died too… as soon I came wandering out, she fell to pieces. When we rolled up that night and I saw you there, it made me think of my mom. I knew I had to go in."

Mary hugs me again. "She's scared."

I nod. "So was I. Being uprooted from home like that isn't easy for any kid." Even a half-demon like me. "It's nice your mother has the space to share."

"Oh, not much space, but we are making do. We are all sharing the room. The insurance will take forever, but Luis has a good lawyer, an' my husband does not give up easy. He's like a dog on a piece of steak." She makes a grabbing-and-pulling gesture, and proceeds to rant about her expectations the insurance will try to come up with some lame excuse to avoid paying.

"Is it all right if I try to talk with her?" I ask.

"Yes, yes. Come." Mary heads for a brown-carpet covered stairwell.

Their room is in the middle on the upper floor. With a twin bed against the left wall, and a small kid-sized mattress on the floor in the other corner, little space remains for anything else. A pair of laundry baskets hold clothes in the far right corner, and a single battered office chair stands by the rear wall where a window isn't. One bad thing about row houses… no side windows. They've got a box fan out in the hall, which helps a little, but it's still stuffy.

Santana's sitting on her bed with her back against the near corner, wearing one of her father's white T-shirts as a dress. A small bottle of nail polish sits by her feet, but her toes are still plain. Her gaze is focused on a point far off beyond the wall she can't see through, and she doesn't react to us walking in. Within a second of looking at her, I get the feeling she wants to avoid being found.

Mary sits on the corner of the twin bed, which is up off the floor on a proper frame. "Santana, honey? Do you remember Miss Amari?"

The girl glances up at me. For a few seconds, I get the most neutral expression imaginable, but then she smiles.

Her mother covers her mouth and draws a surprised breath.

I squat, brace a hand on the rug, and sit on the kid mattress. "Hey, sweetie."

Santana looks down, but manages a weak wave.

"I'm glad you're not hurt."

She swishes her feet back and forth, alternating between a smile and a flat expression.

"You're ten, right?"

Santana nods.

"When I was twelve, my house burned down. I had to live somewhere else too. I didn't have grandparents to stay with, so my mother had to find an apartment. I only saved a couple things to wear, but I didn't let it bother me. Even when other kids made fun of me for being poor. I still had my mom, and we escaped without getting hurt."

Santana looks up at me and smirks.

"Yeah, I know, right? Why should I be scared of fire?" I make a little flappy wings gesture. "I didn't know I was special back then. The fire scared me to death. I don't think you're scared of fire either."

She fidgets and swallows hard before giving me a pleading stare.

"Santana hasn't said a word since that night." Her mother sighs.

No harm embellishing the truth here a little. "I did the same thing for a while too. Maybe a week later, I could talk to my mother, but that's it. Took me months to find a voice at school again." Embellishing... or talking straight out of my ass. Screw it. Not like I'm lying for personal gain here. "When she's ready, she'll talk."

"Yes." Mary rubs her hand back and forth on the bed. "I am so happy she's alive. That she's not talking, how could I complain? Maybe when she's fifteen, it'll be a good thing?"

"I'm pretty good at keeping secrets." I gently take the girl's hand. "I think you're pretty good at keeping secrets too. Some of them are good to not tell."

Santana leans against me.

I ramble for a while about how I felt in the hours and days after the fire, or at least a semi-fictionalized version of the truth where I'd been more frightened. In reality, some of my teachers thought I had serious mental issues due to my lack of emotional reaction, other than not wanting to talk about it. And that came from me being freaked out at not remembering going from surrounded by flames to standing outside in one piece. Every time I mention how my mother was always there for me or busted her ass to keep a roof over our heads and food on the table, I make sure to comment that Mary is doing the same for her.

"I can tell you're scared."

She gazes into nowhere.

"You're worried someone's going to find you."

Santana's eyes go wide. With a gasp, she whips her head around and gawks at me.

"It's true I'm a firefighter and I work for the city. But you know, I'm pretty good at keeping secrets. I think something strange might've happened that night, and you might've seen the man who started the fire. I'd be scared of him too."

She nods, shivering.

I squeeze her hand. "Sometimes secrets are too big to hold all by yourself. Mine's a big secret, and I had to share it with you so I could help. I'm pretty sure yours is big too. If there's someone out there you're afraid is going to hurt you, maybe you can let me help you carry your secret."

"Mama," says Santana in a half-whisper. She stands and moves to sit beside her mother, then pats the bed to her left while looking at me.

Mary grabs her in a hug, rocking her side to side. "Oh, baby. What's got you so frightened?"

When I move to sit next to her on the elevated bed, she again takes my hand, holding her mother's as well. "What I saw happening to you was so much like what'd happened to me. I'm here to help *you*, no matter what you tell me." I try to emulate my mother's reassuring smile. "If you tell me what made you feel guilty, I'll make sure you don't have to worry."

"It was an accident," whispers Santana.

Mary looks at me, dread in her expression.

I raise a calming hand. "I've been a firefighter for about two years. Before that, I was what you'd call a 'free spirit.' Amazed Mom didn't have a full head of grey by the time I got out of high school."

Mary almost laughs, but looks worried.

"Santana." I wait for her to make eye contact. "I'll just put this out there. No one in the department thinks you started the fire. I've been over the scene and I don't think so either, but if you somehow did… it doesn't matter to me. If you can help me understand what happened, I will protect you. No one outside of this room needs to find out."

"I didn't mean to," says Santana.

"Mean to what, baby?" Mary's eyes radiate worry as she rubs her daughter's back. "What happened?"

Santana looks up at me. "I saw a monster and got scared. It was trying to break into our house."

"What?" Mary gasps. "A 'monster?'"

"Yes, Mama. It was like a man, but its eyes lit up like firebugs, and it looked at me real bad. I screamed and put it on fire 'cause I was so scared. It just happened."

Whether it's easier with a child or because of the emotional strength of the memory, I have little trouble poking into Santana's head. I'm still no deep mind reader, but the images and feelings swirling around the uppermost portions of her consciousness are freaky. She's standing in her kitchen, one hand on the fridge door about to open it, when Mr. Nelson—shaggy, hairy, and still quite naked from the morgue—appears in her backyard. Her point of view runs to the window to get a better look. The man senses her and turns, both his eyes glowing bright green. Blood is all over his right hand, and he's sprouted claws, but they're tiny compared to mine, barely an inch.

The vision cuts out as Santana screams.

I pat her hand again. "How did you set it on fire?"

Santana looks down at the rug. "Promise you won't tell Grandma."

"I promise."

She looks up at her mother. "You too, Mama." Tears glide down her cheeks. "I don' want Grandma to hate me."

"Oh, baby. Your grandmother would never hate you." Her mother squeezes her tight again.

"Please," whines Santana, crying even harder. "Say you won't tell her."

"Okay, okay." Mary hugs her. "I promise I won't tell her."

Santana wipes her eyes and lets her arms fall in her lap. A moment later, she finds the courage to speak. "When the monster broke the door, I got scared, so I threw fire on it." She gives her mother a hesitant glance before raising her right hand and summoning a candle flame that dances across her palm. "I can make fire."

The kid's a mage, and summoning fire so young... probably a full-fledged Pyromancer, not a luminare. That explains the shield too... and if a ten-year-old hurled a fire bolt at Mr. Nelson without any training, she's going to be a prodigy.

I squeeze her shoulder, doing my best version of Mom's soothing voice. "Santana, you're not in trouble."

She peers up at me with wide, hopeful eyes. "I'm not?"

"It doesn't sound like you wanted to burn the houses at all."

"No." She shakes her head hard. "The monster... I made the fire go on it like a super soaker, but fire... and it went"—she waves her hands like an explosion—"*whoosh!*"

In her head, the image of the not-quite-right looking Mr. Nelson punches the Rios's back door open. A small arm flies up into the vision and a stream of fire projects from the palm. Nelson goes up like a pile of wet rags soaked in gasoline. In an instant, he's a goddamned conflagration. Wailing and in a panic, he spins around, bumps into the wall, and runs into the yard before crashing through the fence to the right. Santana's vision blurs into a panic-stricken dash to her bedroom.

"I hid in my room, but the fire went everywhere." Santana sniffles. "I couldn't stop it. I tried, but it kept making more. I told the fire to go away, but it wouldn't listen."

Mary, jaw hanging open, turns her gaze to me. "W-what's happening? M-my daughter's a m-mage?"

Santana cringes. "Please don't tell Grandpa and Grandma. They think everything is the devil! They'll hate me!"

I grasp the girl's shoulder. "Santana. Look at me."

She does.

"You did not do anything wrong. That wasn't a person anymore, and he definitely would've hurt you if you didn't defend yourself. The police believe that man started the fire… and in a way, he did." I smile. "I won't say anything about how that man wound up on fire. Thank you for trusting me."

Santana sniffles. "I'm sorry. I tried to make the fire stop, but I'm not good enough."

"It's not your fault. That monster was made out of stuff that burns really fast. You had a choice to do what you did, or do nothing and get hurt. You made the right choice. The police won't bother you. Don't be afraid of getting caught."

The child shrinks in on herself, grinding her big toe into the rug. "That's not what I was afraid of. I'm afraid of my grandparents finding out I got magic… or the monster. I dream about it."

"That monster's gone, sweetie. You got him." I run a hand over her head.

"Baby?" Mary pulls the girl into her lap and hugs her tight. "It don't matter to me you're a mage. I love you no different, and your father's gonna feel the same way. We keep it between us for now."

"Okay." Santana grins and pounces on me with a hug. "Thanks for getting me out of there."

Mary glances at me. "What should I do now?"

I offer a cheesy shrug. "Magic isn't my specialty. I'm more of a psychic. I do know that they've got special schools for gifted kids, like the Academy. That's the biggest one, but it's high-school level. Going to a magic-focused school is optional. I heard they've got scholarships for gifted kids, but you'd have to ask them about it. I, uhh, think Santana's pretty gifted to do what she's doing at her age. She'd probably get a free ride there if she wants to go."

Mary nods.

"My best friend's a mage." I give her the number to Natalie's shop. "I'm sure she'd love to answer your questions."

"Are you gonna go catch the monster?" asks Santana.

"The monster that saw you is quite dead. He can't hurt you anymore… but there's another one out there I need to track down. You just helped me do that."

She grins.

I talk with her for a while about the fire at my mom's trailer, hopefully giving her the tools to mentally put shit back together before I excuse myself—still being on duty, I have to return to the station house. I give them my number too, in case Santana ever needs someone to talk to about watching her home burn down around her.

After another round of energetic thanks from Mary, and a grateful but cautious nod from the grandmother, I leave and go off in search of a secluded spot for takeoff. Emerson's going to *love* this.

No one's stealing his serial killer's bodies… they're just getting up and walking away on their own.

Philly's got a goddamned zombie problem.

14

NECROMANCY

Flying is super convenient. Except for the pain-in-the-ass Elestari. You'd think they own the sky or something. Another one chased me home while whining about my 'being obvious.' But it's just fine for him to fly around in the open, right? Guess it's 'eek! Demon! The world is ending!' thing vs 'aww, look, an angel! A sign from Heaven.' And then some idiot thinks they've been chosen by the divine, believes themselves immortal, and dies an hour later for doing something stupid.

Screw him and his golden wings.

It's the whole cop situation all over again—when I was a kid, they existed to get in the way of my life. I never wanted to hurt anyone, but they like always had a problem with me having fun. What's a little spray paint, right? And the whole weed thing *still* pisses me off. I don't get how alcohol's okay but weed isn't. Who ever heard of someone toking up and beating their wife or going on a pot-fueled rampage with a knife—unless they're slashing open a bag of chips.

Sigh. Money's involved somewhere, I bet.

By the time I land on the roof of my building, Mr. Perfect the Third has put me in a shitty mood. And of course, after spending the past four minutes lecturing me about 'open displays,' the mother-fucker flies brazen as hell back the way we came.

I give his back a double-finger salute as he flies off.

He might have shiny gold feathers and fly faster, but I can make people not see me. Hmm. Maybe I should practice that a bit more. Or I could get a car. Seriously though, the odd cockatrice, centaur, or goblin sneaks into the city every so often and he thinks people will freak out over a girl with wings. And don't even get me started about that twisted thing in South Jersey or the goddamn thunderbirds. If people can handle a hawk the size of a Cessna covered in lightning, they can handle my ass going by overhead.

Grr.

I take two steps toward the door again before middle-fingering the sky at random. In a moment of unbridled rage, I snarl and kick a milk crate someone left lying around. It zooms off into the air and comes down a block and a half away—right through the window of a row house.

Oops.

After I stop laughing, I whistle innocently and make my way inside.

The instant I grab my doorknob, I stop, head hanging. "Fuck. Why did I go home?"

It's only an hour and fifty minutes into my shift and I'm supposed to be at work. Okay, Mr. No-Fly Zone. Suck it. Time to see if I can crank up the mental influence high enough to keep the Elestari from noticing me. Dad said they're almost impossible to affect with our psychic abilities, but I'm pissed enough to try—and late.

The trip to the station house is uneventful, at least until I land behind the building in what I thought was a secluded area by our little tree. After putting my wings away and my polo shirt back on, I start walking for the back door but stop under the weight of a stare.

Lieutenant Sims is there clutching his vape unit, standing at the perfect spot to stay out of sight from the sky under the awning. That's the sad thing about those inhalers... they can't do the hanging off the bottom lip in total shock thing very well. He looks incapable of speech, but his eyes are an obvious WTF.

"Uber's getting expensive," I mutter as I go by.

His gaze tracks me, nothing other than his head moving. That's going to be a fun conversation later, if he bothers. Maybe he'll blank it out of his mind? Here's hoping.

Once I'm inside, I head to the barracks and call Natalie.

"Hey, what's up?" she chirps.

Darn. She's in a good mood. "Sorry."

"What for?"

"You sound happy."

She giggles. "I am. Just got a big job. What are you sorry for?"

"I'm about to ask you a creepy/grim question."

"Oh." She makes a small raspberry noise. "No bigs. What's up?"

"Are zombies real?"

Natalie snickers. "Yeah, they always show up at the polls to vote Corporatist. The Populists are too high to stumble out their door to vote and outnumber them."

"Ha. Ha. I'm serious. I need to know. I saw something—sorta—that I'm pretty damn sure is a legit zombie."

"Hmm." The rustle of her walking comes over the line. "Let me check a couple books. What did you see?"

I tell her about peering into Santana's thoughts, and the odd appearance of Mr. Nelson, specifically the green glowing eyes. "Any luck with that goop yet?"

"Umm. I've heard stories of reanimated dead, but I'm not a necromancer. It's really nasty shit, so I try not to look at it."

I chuckle. "Yeah, movies give you nightmares."

"*One* time!" yells Natalie, playfully angry. "I woke up screaming *once*."

"And everyone on our floor woke up too. The RA thought you were being attacked."

She feigns a sniffle. "I was… by that thing with the bladed glove… so what if it was in my dream. It was scary."

That's Natalie. Twenty-four on the outside, twelve inside.

"Oh, someone I don't trust at all said something that might help."

Page fluttering on her end stops. "Huh? If you don't trust them, why would you think they're trying to help?"

"Because the asshole said it in way that sounded like he was happy I was about to get stuck dealing with a shitty situation. Have you ever heard of a naz-a-duh?"

"Oh, that *does* sound familiar." The loud *slam* of a giant book striking a desk makes me cringe away from the phone. "Hang on."

Lieutenant Sims pokes his head in the door, still with the same WTF look on his face.

"Do you want the truth or just something plausible enough to accept?" I ask.

"Huh?" asks Natalie.

"Not you. Talking to someone here." I hold the phone against my shirt. "This call is part of my helping Detective Zheng."

Sims fidgets at his pockets. "Did I see you with wings... flying?"

"I dunno. Do you want to have seen me with wings?"

"You're not a mage?"

I shake my head. "Nope."

"Will whatever that was cause problems for the department?"

"No way, sir. If anything, it'll help." I smile and give him the big eyes.

Natalie's voice murmurs from the phone.

Sims nods. "Okay. I choose sanity." He pats the doorjamb twice, gives me a lingering look of debate, and walks off.

"Sorry about that," I say into the phone. "Boss."

"Okay, found something. A nazedeh is a kind of reanimated dead person. Apparently, there *are* zombies, or at least magical creations close enough to be basically the same. A nazedeh is a reanimated body where the original soul is trapped inside it."

"Umm. Isn't that basically a zombie?" I make a 'well duh' face at an empty room.

"Not exactly," says Nat. "Zombies don't have souls. They're like the rats of the necromantic world. Raw magical energy is making the corpse move around... like a golem. That's why they're so stupid and slow. Nazedeh are still the same person, only like all tormented and stuff. Umm." A page flips and she mutters random sounds for a few seconds while reading. "Says here they usually go crazy pretty fast. That gunk you gave me was full of necromantic energy, and I'm sure it's blood."

"Are these nazedeh things flammable?" Santana's memory of the thing immolating in a split second replays in my head.

"This book doesn't say, but I did once hear someone at the Academy say that fire is like the best weapon to use on an undead thing, so it's possible."

"Thanks, Nat."

A book thumps closed. "Sure, no problem. Guess all that reading is worth something, after all, Ms. Let's go out and have fun."

"I never said it was useless. I said it was boring." I wink.

"Sure, sure. See you Friday?"

"'Course."

"Later!" she chirps, and hangs up.

Now comes the best part—watching Emerson squirm when I hit him with all this.

A FEW MINUTES TO ONE THAT AFTERNOON, EMERSON PULLS UP. I'M OUT front with McCafferty, Burke, and Herlihy inspecting hoses for damage. It's boring as hell but important—no one likes a leaky fire hose—and it fills time.

I stand as Emerson gets out.

"What'd you do this time?" asks Burke.

"I'm hurt." I give him a fake-wounded pout. "Those days are behind me, Lamar. I haven't been liberty impaired since I was seventeen."

Herlihy chuckles. "So, a couple months ago?"

I roll my eyes, picking at one with my middle finger. "Be right back."

The three stooges erupt in a horrible rendition of the *Cops* theme as I walk over to meet Emerson closer to his car.

"Oh, wow. I get my own music." Emerson waves at them before shifting his attention to me. "So, what's so important you had to tell me in person?"

I grin. "It's not that secret. Mostly, I wanted to see your face."

"That good?"

"That fucked up." Dramatic pause. "Mr. Nelson stole his own body."

Emerson rubs the bridge of his nose. "So you're saying he wasn't dead?"

"He was. Quite dead. You're right. There *is* magic involved. I think your serial killer is a necromancer. The killer isn't stealing the bodies; they're walking off on their own."

His expression of 'you gotta be shittin' me' plus dread plus that itty-bitty trace of 'can I shunt this off on someone else' is worth every bit of making him come here in person. "A necromancer…"

"Yeah. That little girl from the fire saw Nelson, bare-ass-naked, stumbling around in the back yard. She screamed, and I think that startled him into bashing down the fence. Somehow, he wound up inside the next house over. These things are insanely flammable. If the stove was on and he touched it… *foom!*"

"Reanimated dead. Zombies?"

"Not exactly." I share Natalie's explanation of the nazedeh. "Worst-case scenario. Intelligent, strong, tough, and psychopathic. Something about the change makes them go crazy. Nat said they're in continuous torment. Didn't give me any details, but that sounds pretty bad." I gasp mentally. Those ice needles I felt at the morgue… that had to be what he'd been experiencing. Oh ick. Poor bastard.

"Fuck," mutters Emerson.

"Tempting, but I'm seeing someone."

He turns beet red.

I wink. "Teasing. So, how many have been killed so far?"

"Nine." Again, he rubs the bridge of his nose, eyes closed. "All the bodies are still missing, except for one which turned up at the scene of a fire."

"Yeah, I saw them find the guy. That was Nelson… or what was left of him. You got eight of these nazedeh running around the city." I freeze as a weird thought hits me. "Can you charge a dead person with a crime?"

Emerson stares at me. I can't tell if he's stunned I asked that or if he's trying to figure out the answer.

"How were the others killed?"

He shrugs. "All we have are some statements from people who discovered the bodies. None of them remained in the morgue long enough for an autopsy, and the intake photos didn't show any obvious injuries. According to the witnesses, one guy'd been stabbed in the heart, a couple were shot. One victim supposedly had his entire skull mashed open by blunt force, but the photos the ME took show craniofacial damage that may or may not have been fatal."

"Sounds to me like these things regenerate, and depending on how messed up they are, it takes longer for them to get up and walk away."

"The blunt-force guy never even made it to the morgue. Coroner's van was empty except for the body bag when they got back, but the driver said he stopped for coffee on the way, so we think someone hit the van while he was inside."

I scratch my head. "So the most messed up guy is the fastest one to walk away. Ugh. Magic makes no sense."

Emerson frowns at the tarmac. "Welcome to the program. Great. Not only do I have to find a killer, I've gotta deal with effing zombies? How the hell am I going to do that? There've been no reports or sightings. Any idea where these things would hang out?"

"Are there any blood samples?"

"What?" He blinks.

"A psychic thing. I can sometimes locate people if I have a little blood. No idea if it will work on these creatures, but I'll try if you want."

He laughs. "Sure, why not. Your boss okay with me borrowing you again?"

I pivot on my heel to face the station house. "Let me go ask."

15

COVER STORY

Lieutenant Sims looks much better when I duck into his office. He even smiles at me. Guess I won't bring up anything unusual if he doesn't. "Brooklyn?"

"Hi, Ell-tee. Detective Zheng needs the psychic bloodhound again. Is it okay if I go with him? Same deal as last time if a fire happens?"

"Sure. Anything I need to know about?"

"Trying to track down a serial killer preying on the homeless. I think the killer is a necromancer, and one of his victims started the Elmwood fire last week… though unintentionally."

He shivers. "Nothing good'll come of that. Take care of yourself, okay? Necromancy's not bush league."

At the sense of true concern coming from him, I smile with genuine warmth. "Thanks, Ell-tee. Never saw one before, but I'll be as careful as I can."

Sims nods. "Good luck out there."

After a quasi-salute of farewell, I hurry out to Emerson's car and hop in. "Wow. I think I'm breaking some cosmic law of the universe."

"What?" He starts the car and backs out of the fire station driveway.

"Me in the *front* seat of a police car."

Emerson chuckles. "You racked up more time in patrol cars than some rookies get their first year."

"Yeah. I admit I liked it a lot more back when I got free ice cream instead of handcuffs and locked doors."

"Not to pry, but did you ever get it sorted out?"

I tease a bit of hair around my finger, staring at traffic. "Get what sorted out?"

"Whatever was going on in your life that made you act out like that."

"Oh. I guess a bit. I had a lot of pent-up energy and weak impulse control. Spent a lot of time pissed off at the universe that my mother was always so busy, and my dad... That's fixed, at least."

"I'm glad to hear it." He grins while taking a left turn.

My mind drifts off to where I might've wound up if Mom hadn't been superhuman in her niceness... or if Dad had been around all the time. When would he have told me about the Shaar'Nath, or shown me things I can do? Pretty sure I'd have wound up in real jail. I don't *think* I'd have gone psychopath, but minimal impulse control plus feeling superior to humans too young? Yeah, I'd have gotten in shit-loads of trouble. Now, keeping Mom as she is in the equation plus Dad the whole time? That's interesting. Mom's sense of right and wrong with knowing I had... abilities when I lacked the self-control I have now? (Hey, a little is still more than none.)

The car swerving into a parking space snaps me out of my mental wandering.

"Be right back." Emerson hops out and jogs into the police complex.

Yeah. I'm totally cool waiting out here. In fact, I don't even look at the building.

Emerson returns in maybe twenty minutes, carrying a large Ziploc. He slides in behind the wheel and holds it up in two fingers. The big bag holds eight smaller bags, each containing either a scrap of bloody cloth or a small, enchanted phial with a minute amount of liquid blood in it. I bet the magic is preservative in nature. "Please tell me you won't need to open any of these to do your thing."

"The last time I did this, I had the blood on my fingers." I shrug. "I'll try without that. I mean, not like I'm really itching to expose myself to whatever they had." No slam on the homeless, but I don't exactly go running around asking strangers to spit in my mouth either.

"I'd appreciate it." He hands me the bag.

"Feels like I'm drawing victims from a hat." I close my eyes and grab for a small baggie. "First up, scrap of fabric drenched in blood." There's a sharpie-marker case number on the baggie, which doesn't mean anything to me. "It might help if I know a name or who I'm looking for."

Emerson reads the number and punches it in on the car's laptop. The face of an older man with dark skin and a short grey afro pops up on the screen along with case notes. "Lyle Merrick. Age sixty-three. He's been in and out of mental hospitals all his life. Mostly paranoia, but they keep declaring him non-violent."

"Was he?" I ask.

"Looks like it, yeah. Hermetic kinda guy. Kept to himself. He got picked up a couple times for vagrancy, but no criminal history."

"All right, Lyle." I stare at the bag. "Where are you?"

Plastic crinkles between my fingers. Okay, like Dad said. Picture the blood opening like a doorway and push my thoughts into it. A shimmer dances over the saturated fabric, but Emerson doesn't react to it. Oh, awesome. It's working. In my mind, I daydream of diving forward and plunging into the baggie. Tingling spreads across my forehead, and a sense of direction manifests.

"That way." I nod to my right. "It's working. He's there."

Emerson opens the door. "How far?"

"Could be ten feet, could be ten miles."

"That's it?" he asks.

"Yeah." I glance at him. "This isn't exactly zombie Lo-Jack. I don't get a sense of distance, only direction."

He laughs. "Right. Tell me where to turn."

"I can't. I've got a general sense of direction. This is so much easier when flying."

"Flying?"

Oops. "In theory. Don't s'pose you can get a chopper?"

"Not for a voodoo project." He waits a few seconds for an opening and pulls out into traffic.

This seriously would be *much* faster to do alone. But... yeah. I'm not explaining that to a cop. They can't accept the idea that people can be responsible with weed; I don't trust what they'd think of the real me.

My sense of direction pulling me toward Lyle Merrick creeps farther to my right. "I think he's pretty close. The direction is changing fast. Turn right when you can."

At the end of the block, we pull a turn that puts the feeling mostly in front of me, but still off to the right.

"Okay. Keep going straight for a while."

A few minutes, and blocks, later, the sense begins to slip right again.

I point at the next cross street. "Another right."

This sends the pull swerving past front and hovering a little left, inching around as we drive.

"Slow down. We're real close. The direction's changing fast. That alley."

Emerson hangs a left, nosing into a gap between buildings almost too tight for the car. This definitely looks like a bad area. After maybe sixty feet of rolling along at a walking pace, the draw toward Mr. Merrick slides to a point directly left of me.

"Stop. He has to be around here somewhere."

"What exactly are we looking for?"

"Lyle Merrick," I deadpan while opening the door as much as the wall allows and slithering out of the car. "Other than that, probably a mess."

"Great." Emerson grumbles and does the limbo as well.

I walk around the front of the car and enter a narrow doorway in the side of a crumbling brick building that leads to a dingy corridor. The stench of piss, garbage, and chemical foulness is enough to water my eyes. Peeling pea-green paint scrawled with black graffiti covers both walls. Two naked lightbulbs hang on wires from holes in the ceiling. Doors line both sides, suggesting this place was (or maybe still is) an apartment building.

"Careful," whispers Emerson while drawing his Glock. "I don't like the look of it here."

"Bet the rent's reasonable. Looking for a new apartment?"

He stifles a chuckle.

"Someone's using e-meth."

Emerson makes the same face as the cop who picked me up at eight for wandering around alone when I told him I hadn't eaten all day. "I'm sorry you know what that smells like."

I've dabbled with peyote, mushrooms, LSD, E, Sylph, and even Glimmerfaerie, and I'm *all* about weed... but e-meth? Fuck that. "I was wild, not stupid. Idiots made that shit around where I grew up. I got a nice good whiff of it when a cookery exploded and took out my childhood home."

"Ouch."

At the end of the hall, I notice a downward tug on the magical sense. "Basement. I think we're right on top of him."

Emerson nods and scoots past me, raising his weapon. I follow him around a corner and past three apartments before he finds the main stairwell and takes it down. Old needles, used-up lighters, condoms, and all manner of bottles litter the landing.

Even with boots on, I don't feel safe here. "Ugh. Careful. Don't step in AIDS."

He looks back at me, shakes his head, and continues. "You know that's blown way out of proportion for politics, right? Lifemages can cure it easily."

"Yeah, but most of the poor fuckers who get it can't afford that."

Emerson stops at the bottom and listens by a heavy brown-painted steel door. "There's a Lifemage at the basilica in Center City. I'm pretty sure he doesn't charge a dime."

"Huh. Really?"

He gives me a 'shh' gesture, and nudges the door open.

The basement is dark, cavernous, and heavy with the stink of mildew. A little light leaking in from the door reveals the corner of a big-ass boiler, and some stacked cardboard boxes. Holy shit, this place is straight out of a horror movie. Most alarming is the mushy squishing noise emanating from deep inside.

I grab Emerson's shoulder. When he looks back, I mouth, "Do you hear that?"

He nods and eyes the floor as if to say 'wait here.'

Screw that.

When he gets a few steps ahead, I creep after him. I'm pretty sure a Glock is going to do jack shit to a nazedeh, unless he stuffs it up the thing's nose and the muzzle flare happens to light it on fire. Once he edges past the scary-as-hell boiler, he stops and pulls out a small flashlight. The squishing sounds like it's coming from the most distant corner on the left. Emerson heads toward it, stepping around a busted air conditioner next to a couple mattresses soaked in awfulness. Scraps of particleboard and smashed small appliances wink in and out of view in the tiny flashlight beam.

I clamp my hand over my mouth as an overpowering urge to vomit comes out of nowhere. My eyes water, but I manage to hold it in and keep quiet. Seconds later, the conscious realization of a horrible stench pierces my awareness. Something dead and rotting is down here.

Emerson gags, but continues advancing until a rusting workbench comes into view. The tools littering it look like they're from the sixties, and have been sitting there since. I half-expect to see a dismembered body chained to a table given the feel in the air down here.

Slurping joins the ongoing distant squishing. Oh, boy. I bet this is going to be nasty.

My hip catches the end of the workbench, rattling it and knocking something metal over with a *clank*. Emerson jumps and spins back, evidently not having noticed I'd followed. His initial 'dammit, I told you to stay put' expression changes to a look of relief a second later at not being alone. He's borderline freaking out. I can't blame him. This isn't like walking into a fire… I'm on edge too.

I gulp back my nerves and nod reassuringly.

He mouths, "He's right around here."

Again, I nod.

Emerson raises his weapon and flashlight and takes a rapid step left around the end of the workbench/cabinet. His flashlight beam lands on a pair of men. A lanky guy in a filthy brown jacket sits with his back against the wall, a vacant expression on his face and a long tendril of drool falling from his lips. Lyle Merrick, his dark shirt blackened with blood, kneels next to him, chewing at a hole in the other guy's skull—the source of the squishing.

It's so utterly disgusting, I can't help but laugh. "Wow. I thought that brain thing was made up."

Merrick snarls and whips his head up, his face covered in fresh blood. Both of his eyes glow pale green, but they're still solid eyeballs. Hah. I'm cooler. Mine turn into energy.

"Get on the ground," says Emerson.

"He's not going to listen." I shake my head. "He's already dead."

Merrick continues growling, and rises to his feet.

"On the fuckin' ground *now!*" shouts Emerson.

When Merrick takes a step, the Glock goes off with a deafening report and a near-blinding flash. I can't tell if the bullet hit. Roaring, the nazedeh charges at Emerson, who fires twice more in rapid succession, but the thing-that-used-to-be-Merrick doesn't slow down.

With a grunt, I lunge sideways and shoulder block Emerson out of the way. Merrick's wild fist rams into my side; my arm gives out with a loud *crack*. Standing becomes sliding in an instant. My head plows a trench in bottles, cans, and cardboard junk.

Ow. Son of a bitch. "Grr."

"Brooklyn!" shouts Emerson.

Muzzle flare lights up the dark about twenty feet away for an instant, the pyro-flower image lingering on my retinas for a few blinks after. Ooh, that undead fucker's strong. Two points of green light swivel toward where Emerson's voice came from. The instant I catch sight of Merrick's glowing eyes, I focus my telekinesis on him and yank with as much force as I can exert.

The dead man flies off his feet, smashing into the concrete floor with a wet, splattery squish. A faint throb of discomfort washes over my brain. Well, Dad, I guess I *can* splatter brains with a thought. Not quite as clean as you though. I had to go through the skull to get to the soft parts.

Crunching comes from my arm, bones grinding back into place. Threads of pain leap across the back of my hand, trading places with numbness. Every time the bones scrape, an answering twitch happens in my fingers. Crap, this itches. I grit my teeth and muffle a growl of irritation. Muzzle flash goes off another three times, at a downward angle.

Damn, that's loud. I cringe.

"It's not stopping him… he's still fuckin' moving!" shouts Emerson.

I roll flat on my back, seeing stars from the pain/itch/weirdness in my right arm. "What part of *zombie* didn't you get?"

"I already shot it in the head. It's not working!"

Merrick emits a distorted moan. The squelching of wet flesh reaching my ears conjures a mental image of his skull mushing back together. Hmm. This was the blunt force trauma guy, right? Guess he's used to that.

I scramble back to my feet and rush over by Emerson who's got his flashlight trained on Merrick's re-inflating head.

"Don't freak out." I raise both my hands toward the moving dead man.

"Oh, I'm a bit past that point already," mutters Emerson. "Goblins I can deal with. *This?*"

"Heh."

I concentrate on the way Dad taught me to pull the flame straight out of Imbreleth, our home dimension. The warm tingle starts deep in my gut, rising up within my chest to my arms. When the sensation reaches my palms, dark crimson fire streams over Merrick. I cringe a little at the heat I generate, like gripping a fresh cup of Starbucks without that little cardboard sleeve.

Faster than I can even think *die!*, the body conflagrates like I touched a lit match to a wad of tissue paper soaked in ethanol. Emerson yowls and jumps back, but the wave of heat is way milder than what I summoned. Thankfully, nazedeh burn normal. "Whoa…"

I run around kicking cardboard boxes or anything else that catches back at the corpse, trying to contain the burn as much as possible.

Merrick yowls with a strangling, gurgling cry, thrashing and struggling to leap at me. Glowing fluid sprays out from dozens of places where his skin ruptures, spurting bright green napalm more than ten feet in random directions. I hold him down with telekinesis, so he doesn't run around like a headless flaming chicken, setting this whole damn building alight.

He stops twitching after maybe eight seconds and simply burns.

"Be right back," mutters Emerson.

I keep circling and corralling anything on fire into a pile. A minute or two later, Emerson runs back over (at least we have light from the fire) with a small extinguisher and sprays Merrick's remains until we're once again in the dark.

"What. The fuck. Was that?" asks Emerson.

"A nazedeh."

He spots his flashlight on my chest. "No. I mean the fire thing."

"I work for the *fire* department… they teach us that in the second month."

Emerson smirks.

"Psychic fire." I try the 'trust me' smile. "And no, I did not burn down my mom's trailer. E-meth lab two lots over exploded. I only learned this trick a week or so ago."

"Really?" He shakes his head. "Psychic fire? Never heard of anything like that."

"Worked, didn't it?"

He looks me up and down. "You okay? That thing got quite a piece of you." The flashlight beam settles on my right arm, but it's only dirty and scuffed.

"I have a regeneration amulet."

"How could you have possibly afforded one of those?" he asks.

"Oh. Good point." I put a finger on my lip and strike a thinking pose. "I should probably come up with a better excuse than that or I'll have people trying to mug me."

"Brooklyn?"

"Hmm?" I ask in a sweet tone.

"That thing swatted you across the basement and you're not even bruised. You knocked me on my face, and you did that fire thing."

"Yeah." Sigh. How the crap do Elestari keep their secrets? Oh, right. They cheat. They can magic people to forget shit. If this keeps up, I'll need to stop doing nice things for people. "Guess I'm special."

"Is there something going on in your life you need help with?"

I blink at him. Wow. He's still trying to save the lost, rebellious little girl. I'm not quite her anymore. Though, every now and then, I miss it. This whole adulting thing is overrated. Responsibility's a big bag of suck. "Nothing you can help with."

"Some problems sound a lot bigger in your head. Talking about them can make them seem not so overwhelming."

"Wow, Emerson..." I chuckle. "I'm not some abused teen. I could tell you, but..."

He cocks his head back. "You'd have to kill me?"

I roll my eyes. "Ugh. That line's as overdone as Merrick. I could tell you, but you'd either think I'm crazy or start drinking yourself blind every night."

"That bad?"

"There's no such thing as angels or demons. They're both extra-planar creatures from another dimension who created our world as a wall to stop themselves from wiping each other out."

He stares at me.

"Feeling a little itch for vodka yet?"

"So... I'm guessing you're part not-demon?"

I laugh. "Taking 'little hellion' a bit too literally, are we?"

"Well, your juvenile record speaks for itself... but aside from that, your little fire show was dark. Your Mom's in the system, but there's no mention whatsoever of a father."

"What? It wasn't dark. Merrick was already dead. I can't help it if fire's the only way to kill them." I frown at the smoking corpse. "Again."

Emerson chuckles. "I meant dark as in color. Fire isn't usually that deep shade of crimson. Your chi is the same, perhaps even calmer. You aren't as scared as you used to be."

Grr. I wasn't scared as a kid. I was... uninhibited. "Why, Emerson Zheng... you're psychic?" I flutter my eyelashes at him.

"I've been referred to as 'sensitive' before, but never psychic." He walks over to the man Merrick had been eating. "What am I gonna call this one in as?"

I raise an eyebrow. "Bath salts?"

He shakes his head. "Not funny."

"Would they believe drugs more or less than zombie attack?"

He sighs. "We had a zombie thing go on years ago. I was still on patrol. This kid in Mayfair figured out he had mage abilities... necromancy. Bad situation. Always had an off kinda air around him, yanno. Not a good combination when someone's got that kind of ability plus they turn out to be a sociopath."

"Ugh. A kid?"

"Well, he was young to me. Think he was seventeen when he decided to take the city apart. Got tired of being picked on at school for being 'the creepy loner.'" He pulls out his cell and calls in a crime scene unit.

I roam around looking for embers, making sure the fire's all the way out. "What happened to him?"

"Last I heard, he's in a mental ward still."

"Poor kid."

"He'd be almost thirty now."

"Still. Shitty way to live." I step on a smoking bit of cardboard and grind my boot into the ground. "So. You ready to do this seven more times?"

He moans, hanging his head.

MY SENSE LEADS ME TO THE NEXT NAZEDEH NEAR (FITTINGLY ENOUGH) Hunting Park in a construction site at the corner of North 16th Street and West Roosevelt Boulevard. It's a big lot, and looks like they're renovating a store to the point they've torn it down entirely. We make our way past the temporary fence surrounding the property and creep in among piles of smashed concrete and the deep ruts of dump truck tires. They're still in the process of carting away the old building, though some naked steel framework is already standing at the back end. Guess the developer's in a hurry.

"Why's this place shut down in the middle of the day?" I ask.

Emerson shrugs one shoulder, keeping his Glock up. "Maybe our friend scared them off?"

"Yeah, maybe. Why are you bothering with the gun?"

"Habit. Makes me feel better."

Metal clatters in the distance like a stack of pipes falling over. I point toward it. Emerson nods and goes that way. Sigh. Stupid chivalric bastard. What's he hoping to do? The second he leans around the end of a pile of concrete rubble, a familiar gurgling snarl comes from the other side.

Emerson lets out a yelp and scrambles backward.

The former Mr. Wayne C. Riley (another veteran like Nelson) runs out, heading for Emerson. There are few things in this world that I want to touch less than a fifty-plus undead naked homeless man with nipple-length greasy hair. Fresh blood smears his ghastly pale chest, one patch a clear handprint. Grunting and huffing, he barrels toward Emerson, who shoots him a few times in the chest, but it doesn't slow the guy down in the least.

I take a step to intercept, but hesitate because... he's flapping. Eww. No wanty touchy.

Riley rushes past me, reeking of whiskey vomit, feces, and sharp chemical fumes like industrial solvent. Highly flammable industrial solvent.

Emerson screams and runs.

Dammit. I grab telekinetic hold of the dead guy and drag him to the ground backward. He rolls ass-over-head in a somersault and springs to his feet facing me. Without missing a beat, he raises his hands and rushes at me like he'd forgotten Emerson existed.

Ugh. I scoot to the side, leading him a few paces while hunting for something… anything I can use not to have to touch this guy. He closes in and swings to take my head off, but between a telekinetic shove at his body and me diving to the side, I avoid it. Mr. Riley smashes a concrete chunk hard enough to crack it and leave a splat of the same bright green liquid when his hand turns to mush.

That seems to have registered some kind of pain, as he stops and stares mystified at his regenerating limb. I spot a tangle of rebar jutting out of a nearby mound of debris, which would work wonderfully to keep him from starting a major fire. In the second I'm distracted by that, Riley hurls himself into a leap, trying to tackle me, but I keep my footing. He winds up grabbing me in a bear hug that forces me backward a few steps as I crane my neck to keep his teeth away from my face.

Ugh. Eww. *It's* touching my leg.

I cringe, sprout claws, and sink my fingers into his chest to grab hold before spinning and hurling him at the rubble as hard as I can throw. He flies chest first onto the tangle of steel rods, which burst like porcupine quills from his back with a spray of glowing green blood.

Emerson gawks at me.

Shit. Can't a girl keep a secret for once?

I walk the twenty or so feet over to where the nazedeh is struggling, but hopelessly stuck, and light him on fire before sticking my hands into it to burn the disgusting crud from my fingers. Riley wails and howls, wrenching his body hard enough to bend some of the rebar in the several seconds he has before the conflagration destroys him. The whole time I stand there letting my fingers burn clear, Emerson's mouth hangs open.

"I need an adult," I whine.

"What?" Emerson stumbles over.

"Can I show you on a doll where that old, nasty man touched me?" I point at my hip. "Zombie penis made contact."

Emerson levels his finger off at me. "I never want to hear those two words in that particular order ever again."

I laugh. "You and me both. Guess this guy's a morgue escapee. There's probably a dead construction worker around here somewhere."

"Yeah. This is a damned mess."

"We're cleaning it up. Good thing they're being shy."

Emerson paces around, shaking his head. "Who knows how many victims there've been. I don't suppose you know how often they feel a need to kill?"

"Not a clue. I'm no mage."

He puts his hands on his hips. "What are you?"

"Brooklyn." I flash 'cheesy smile.' "Really, I'm still the same person you arrested eight years ago, only with slightly bigger boobs and a little more maturity."

"Wayward teens don't throw grown men that far with enough force to impale them on rebar."

I shrug and point at the smoldering Mr. Riley. Hah. 'The Smoldering Mr. Riley' would make an awesome name for a band. "He's skinny."

"Yeah." Emerson sighs at the clouds. "I'm in over my head."

"Me too… only not with this case." I sigh. "Okay, you wanna know?"

"Do I?" he asks.

"I really don't want to wind up reclassified as a magical creature and banned from the city."

"You can talk. You're not a creature."

"Goblins can talk."

He laughs. "Yeah, but barely."

"Fine. You were right the first time. I'm half not-demon, but didn't know it until like a month ago. No, I'm not evil. Demons aren't what you think."

Emerson smacks his lips, glances at the burning corpse, and nods. "Okay. I'll file that away for now."

"Really?" I raise both eyebrows in surprise, not only at what he said, but at his actual intention to keep my secret. "That's a lot easier than I thought it would be."

"Before I came to ask you for help, I looked over your juvenile records. It's all typical kid bullshit—just a lot of it. If you had it in you to be evil, I think it would've shown itself already."

Flashes of Frank's last few seconds of life glide by in my thoughts and a wry grin spreads over my face. "Oh, I'm a perfect angel."

He snorts into a laugh. "So, do you like have horns?"

"I can if I want to."

"Wow. Shit. We better get moving before these dead guys kill more people. For now, I guess 'psychic fire' works as a cover story if anyone asks."

I bat my eyelashes at him. "You say the sweetest things, Detective Zheng."

"Let me call this one in." He stares at the dead man for a few seconds before pulling out his phone. "Damn. I really hate zombies."

16

MOP UP

We hone in on the fifth nazedeh hiding out in a thickly wooded area at the south end of FDR Park, where the terrain's too thick for a car. Emerson's decided to use his brain and carries a flare gun. Worked great on the last one we found in an alley downtown. Also, much less tiring on me not having to summon fire. The sun's starting to weaken in the sky, but we've still got a couple hours of daylight left. For no particular reason, I ramble about my father and the whole Armistice thing. I even make him laugh by explaining my first horrible attempt at flying.

"Whoa," says Emerson once I stop babbling. "That's quite a weight to carry."

"Relax. There's no way I'm ever going to do what they want." I nod a little to the left. "That way. You know, I'm not really sure why I just up and dumped all that on you at once. Guess I'm still scared of lying to the cops."

"That never stopped you before."

"Touché." I hop across a small stream. "Yeah, but only until I got nabbed. Once I wound up in the car, I was straight with you guys. No sense making shit worse for myself at that point. Thank my mom for that, by the way. She tried to keep me centered despite my impulse control issues. I don't think I did anything *really* bad. Drinking and fiddling around with drugs were probably the worst."

A *snap* in the distance makes him stop. He raises the flare gun. "What's the most illegal thing you've ever done?"

Killed a guy for trying to rape a child. Which… isn't exactly bad. Might not be illegal, even. Still not gonna tell him that. Somehow I doubt he'd let it slide. "Probably when I shoplifted a PlayStation 2. Or maybe covering the police chief's car with spray painted penises."

Emerson snickers. "I remember that. You know they still sometimes draw them on things to piss him off."

I gasp into a laugh. "Really?"

"Yeah, some of the guys zoomed in on one from the evidence photo of the car, printed out a bunch, and wallpapered his office."

My hand over my mouth doesn't do much to quiet my laughter.

A snarl from the weeds up ahead startles us both silent. We exchange a glance. Emerson nods toward the spot and circles to the left.

"Oh, what was that noise?" I deadpan. "I hope there's nothing dangerous out here."

Another twig snap comes from up ahead, farther away. Wow. Is this one running?

I point toward the moving rustle.

Emerson advances in a cautious combat stance, flare gun trained.

Glowing green eyes appear in the bushes a short distance away from him. The greying form of Pedro Luna stands into view, cringing away from us. Two knives stick out of his chest, and a huge shard of glass hangs from the side of his neck, dripping green blood. His ass-length ponytail swishes when he spins fast to face Emerson. He grunts, staring at the flare gun.

Whoa. I'm getting a feeling of intent from it/him. He wants us to kill him.

"What's with this one… not attacking?" asks Emerson.

Luna gurgles, lowering his arms and sticking his chest out.

"He wants you to kill him. Must be in a shitload of pain."

The dead man convulses, mashing himself in the head a few times before glaring at me.

"Mental pain?"

"Who did this to you?" asks Emerson.

Luna moans incoherently while waving his arms around.

"I thought you said they still had their souls."

I glance at him. "They do, but that doesn't mean their bodies work. He's not really breathing anymore, so I guess talking's a pain in the ass… and that giant piece of glass in his throat."

Luna makes a finger gun, yanks his hand back in a suggestion of recoil, and pats himself on the chest. He repeats the magey hand-waving. Yeah, great. Thanks. We knew that much already.

"What did he look like?" I ask. "White guy?"

The shard of glass slides out from Luna's neck as he nods. He collapses to one knee, grabbing his head, and emits a long, moan while his whole body shudders. Ouch, poor guy. That looks painful.

"Was the man who killed you old? Young?" I ask.

A disconcerting growl of anguish breaks the silence. Luna grabs at his hair, two fistfuls pulling until his scalp begins to peel away. His head snaps up a second later, a feral gleam in his eyes.

I shake my head and take a step back. "Guess we used up all his minutes. These zombies must have a cheap plan."

Luna roars and springs upright. Emerson fires; an orange flare streaks across the few yards separating them and burrows into the dead man's chest. Luna goes up like a torch. Screeching, he flails his arms about and darts off in a random direction. Before he can get too far, I telekinetically levitate him. My pyrotechnic piñata screams and spews goo. Dribbles of his unnatural blood spatter to the ground, starting small fires in the dirt. Thankfully, the ground is damp enough that they don't spread far.

A few minutes later when the flames sputter out and I'm sure he's dead—well, dead-er—I release my telekinetic hold. The charred skeleton hits the ground with a crunch like a bundle of thin twigs.

"Poor guy."

Emerson cracks the flare gun open and slides another shell in.

"This is pretty damn far from what I imagined I'd be dealing with when I got the idea to try for detective."

"You *can* live your dreams," I say in a flat tone and wander over to where Mr. Luna had been hiding, but find only a bottle of cheap whiskey and the most rancid-smelling puddle of vomit I've ever encountered. My eyes water in an instant. After throwing fire on the puddle (which catches like a gasoline spill) I stagger away, gagging.

"You okay?" Emerson pulls out his phone.

"Holy shit, that stinks." I cough, bile trailing off my lip. "Like someone made a cadaver smoothie."

Emerson gurgles, holding his stomach.

Ugh. I spit a few times and gulp fresh air. Guess nazedeh don't get along well with booze. By the time Emerson finishes requesting a crime scene unit to our location, I'm back to normal. His phone rings within ten seconds of him putting it away. He sighs and pulls it back out.

"Zheng," says Emerson to the phone. After a murmur from the other end, the irritation in his expression shifts to alarm. "Shit. All right. Do *not* remove the body from the scene, and have at least two officers keep an eye on it." He pauses, listening. "Yes, I'm serious. And make sure one of them has a flare gun. On the way as soon as I can. Waiting on a body pickup." He pauses for a second. "Yes, a flare gun."

"Another victim?" I ask.

"Yeah." He clicks his phone off and grumbles at the trees. "Downtown."

Damn, it's edging up on 8:00 p.m. Worse, I'm not even remotely hungry. Wow, and I thought fire department hours sucked. We stand around swapping stories of long shifts. His getting a 3:45 a.m. wake-up call about a case beats my midnight page for a fire alarm.

As soon as the flashlights of a pair of patrol officers leading the crime scene group emerge out of the trees to our north, Emerson jogs over, points at the body, and rushes off to the car.

17

ANOTHER LOST SHADOW

Of all the time I've spent in police cars throughout my life, I've never been in one before when they ran code 3. Though, I must say the seating is way more comfortable without handcuffs. It's surreal to watch traffic move out of our way. In the fire truck, you get the occasional asshole who doesn't yield. They regret it if they pull that shit when I'm there. At least if there's no kids in the car. Last guy was a gold Audi who I guess thought himself too important to suffer a twenty-second delay in his trip. I left his pretentious piece of shit on the side of the road upside down. Scared the shit out of Cortez, who was driving our rig.

Heh. To this day, they think the guy hit something and flipped it.

"How long do these things take to get back up?" asks Emerson.

I shrug. "You'd be much better off asking a necromancer. Or even a mage. My best trick is being immune to fire."

Emerson laughs. "Oh, I get it now."

"What?"

"Of course. Why you joined the FD. Makes total sense."

I clutch the overhead handle during a hard left turn. "Ever since the trailer fire, I've felt a pull. Never understood why. I even blanked the memory of crawling out and not burning. Didn't get that back until like a month ago."

"So, anyway." Emerson swerves around a filthy box truck, siren wailing. "I'd like you to come to the scene and see if you can get any visions or whatever."

"Well." I make a show of looking around at the car. "Since I seem not to have much choice in where we're going at the moment, sure."

He shoots me a worried glance for an instant until he sees me grinning. "Sorry."

"Don't be. I'm thoroughly conditioned to do whatever cops tell me."

"I wish the *actual* criminals had that attitude."

"Are you calling me like a criminal-lite or something?" I chuckle.

"No, I see it now. Inside, some part of you knew you weren't like everyone else. The dichotomy of it made you restless. Now I feel a bit guilty over all the time you spent with us."

Shrug. "Eh. I'm over it. Only really bothered me once."

"Once?" he asks as we dart through a red light. "Want to talk about it?"

"Nothing really bad happened. Just my first time not sleeping in my own bed. Pulled an overnight in a cell when I was eleven. I'm pretty sure that's the only time I'd been genuinely terrified. Didn't know if I'd ever see my mother again." I sigh into an eye roll. "'Course, by the time I was fourteen, it felt more like spending the night at a friend's house."

"Why did you keep getting in trouble?"

I wait for another hard turn to finish. "Remember what I said about my not having much impulse control? If something looked fun, I did it. That whole 'ability to contemplate consequences of my actions' didn't really form in my head until like, oh, a month ago. Probably why I'm sitting here right now."

"This is *fun* to you?"

"Fun enough... and I suppose it won't hurt for me to do something helpful once in a while."

He kills the siren and slows as we approach a cluster of marked police cars, lights ablaze. "Here we are."

After he noses in to park by the mouth of an alley, we get out and approach a cluster of uniformed officers. Two older cops give me the 'do I know you?' stare. I wave at them as we walk past. A short distance in from the street, the body of a woman is sprawled out on her back by a pair of green dumpsters. She's late thirties maybe, and filthy, with scraggly hair that could be light brown or dark blonde. Three large canvas shopping bags lay nearby, also covered in grime, as are her two jackets, sweatshirt, and jeans.

A patrol sergeant with little tufts of grey over his ears in his otherwise black hair stands guard over the deceased. Another cop who I'm sure is younger than me hovers back a step, looking ready to throw up at any moment.

"What's the story here?" asks Emerson.

The older cop nods at the body. "Locals called in a gunshot. Found this one lying here. Couple of business owners we talked to knew her as 'Norma Jean.' Thought she worked for Avon or something. Always running around with bags full of shampoo and shit. Real name's Catherine Henry. We picked her up a couple times, mostly shoplifting from salons around here."

"Area vagrants called her Rambles," adds the younger cop. "Said she never stopped talking."

We all stare at each other in silence for a few seconds.

"She's not talking much now," I mutter.

The cops blink at me.

"Oh, come on. Someone was gonna say it. I did it so you guys don't have to feel guilty about making the tasteless crack you all thought of." I crouch near the body. "Maybe she's still got some things to say."

"Who's that?" asks the older cop.

"Sergeant Allen, you don't remember me?" I lift my head and give him my super-innocent face.

He blinks, fires off a WTF glance at Emerson, and erupts in laughter. "The chief's car… that was awesome."

"Huh?" the younger cop looks between us, confused.

Once Sergeant Allen stops laughing, he nods at Emerson. "What's she doing here?"

"I'm trying to get a psychic read on the vic."

Allen shakes his head, still chuckling. "If she's psychic, she ain't a good one. Never saw us coming."

"Right," I mumble. "Not that kind of psychic. I don't do the future thing."

Emerson squats on the other side of the dead woman. "Hmm. Bullet hole and bloodstains on the sweatshirt."

"We'll know it's your guy if there's no wound under it." I say.

"Where's the ME?" Emerson looks around.

Sergeant Allen shrugs. "Figured they'd get here before you."

"I need to touch the body. Is the forehead okay, or will that ruin evidence?"

Emerson leans down to examine the woman's grime-smeared face. "Should be okay. Gloves?"

"If only. I think they'll get in the way." I look up at him. "If the imprint's strong, I might involuntarily re-enact being shot. If I fling myself to the ground, don't panic."

Both patrol officers look on with keen interest.

Well, here goes.

I gingerly place two fingers on the woman's forehead, close my eyes, and open my mind.

The vision hits me fast, as seen from Rambles' eyes. A constant stream of incomprehensible muttering goes by in the back of my head. Something about taxi cabs, the president, and griffon eggs. She mutters continuously about nonsense while picking among trash. After a moment, she seizes a giant white bottle of hair conditioner and holds it up like she's unearthed a gold statuette from Incan ruins.

Motion at the corner of her eye draws her attention to a man on the older side of twenty, with a narrow face and light brown hair, short and neat. He's in a nice long coat, also brown. Between his warm smile, fancy clothes, and that he's made eye contact with her, she figures him a promising mark for begging.

My point of view takes a step closer. The continuous flow of words in the back of her mind leaks out to muttering speech about taxes, how some place nearby conspires with the CIA to reduce the size of their cheeseburgers while charging the same price, and something about nylon.

The man pulls a gun, still smiling, and fires without a word.

Pain takes all the breath from my lungs. We collapse together to the ground, gazing up past the concrete canyon around us at the late afternoon sky. Fluid fills my throat; hot blood splashes on my cheeks with each attempt to take a breath that won't happen. The killer stoops over me, tucking his gun back into his coat. He's sporting an expression mixing condescension with concern, like he's just hit a dog with his car and thinks taking it to the vet absolves him of any guilt.

He presses his hand down on my chest, muttering under his breath. Whitish, vaporous light appears in a whorl around his arm, flowing into me with a cool numbness. The agony of the gunshot races upward and away, as if an impaling sword had been yanked free. My head rolls back, muscles refusing to move. Blue sky and clouds fill my vision as an overwhelming sense of frustration radiates from the man.

Another flash of eerie white light happens beyond the edge of my vision. His anger grows, consuming me too. The psychometric vision shifts. I'm no longer the victim, but the killer. A snarl leaks between my teeth like I've been playing the same level in a video game for fourteen hours straight, and for only the second time got close to finishing it only to die to a cheap gimmick.

"Brooklyn!" shouts Emerson, shaking me out of the vision.

Both cops are staring at me; the younger one has a hand on his gun.

I catch myself baring my teeth at Emerson, my breathing ragged, the idea of pounding him feels like a good one.

"Brook?" He raises a hand. "What's up? You're, uhh, growling."

The vicarious anger falls away, and I slump forward, eyes closed. "Sorry. I'm not pissed off… that came from the killer."

"Uhh," says Sergeant Allen. "Do I wanna know why you sounded like a fuckin' grizzly bear?"

"Psychic stuff," mutters Emerson as he dusts my back off. "So... what happened? Guess you got a vision here?"

It takes me another minute or so to collect my thoughts back to myself. "Oh yeah. I saw the guy."

"Let me record you?" Emerson takes his phone out.

"Sure."

Once he hits the button, I recount the vision in as much detail as I can. "This necromancer doesn't know his magic is working. He's incredibly pissed. I think he's *trying* to make nazedeh or something, and the bodies aren't getting up right away, so he thinks it's failing. He cast another spell on her after she'd died, but it didn't do anything. All that growling... sorry. His anger affected me."

"Wow. I'd hate to see you truly pissed off." Emerson stops the recording.

Yeah, that's not a pretty picture. I really hope Ashley didn't watch me rip that shithead apart. I guess since she doesn't wet herself as soon as she sees me, she didn't witness the grisly details. Good. That makes me feel better. And yeah, I'd shred Frank all over again, no regrets.

"So now what?" I ask.

Emerson dials a number and raises his phone to the side of his head. "Well... we wait for the ME, and maybe you can work with a sketch artist."

I stand, dusting alley funk off my hands. The unspoken part of that is we're going to be staying with this woman until she gets back up.

At 9:42 p.m., I follow a medical examiner, Emerson, and an assistant ME into a procedure room. Emerson and I hang back a short distance while the doctor and his assistant move Rambles' body onto the metal table and begin cutting her clothing off. The assistant is young, maybe still in school—an intern perhaps? For once, I don't feel so alarmingly pale. This girl's nearly as white as me, with almost the same shade of jet hair.

The doctor keeps giving us (mostly Emerson) nasty looks. He's throwing off irritation, both at us being in here and at his being disturbed 'after hours.' Emerson used the excuse that the serial killer has stolen all the bodies of his victims so far before they could be examined to explain both the rush, and why we're observing the autopsy.

Article by article, the ME team removes the woman's clothing and puts each item in a plastic bag after photographing it. A deformed bullet falls to the floor when they pull her innermost sweatshirt off. The assistant retrieves and bags it. Stains in various shades of burgundy, yellow, and brown mottle Rambles' skin along with dozens of red marks on her arms and thighs. I can't tell if they're insect bites, needle marks, or something else. While the assistant ME draws blood, the doctor maneuvers around the body, taking pictures and narrating to an overhead microphone about every mark, blemish, bruise, or stain he finds.

A tedious half hour later, the assistant ME pushes a cart with trays and tools over. The doctor grabs a large scalpel and rests his left hand on the dead woman's chest.

"Beginning examination of internal organs. Initial incision at 10:13 p.m."

He presses the scalpel down near the right collarbone to start the huge Y-shaped cut. As soon as the blade sinks beneath the skin, a spritz of luminous green fluid spatters over the doctor's chest. Rambles' eyes snap open—glowing the same shade if bright emerald.

"Shit!" I yell.

The doctor looks up from the cut to glare at me for making noise.

Rambles arm flies from the table and seizes the doctor by the throat. The assistant ME screams, dropping the large metal tray she'd been holding ready to receive the first organ. I rush forward, grabbing the woman's hand and trying to pry it away from the doctor's neck as his face turns reddish-purple. Blood seeps out from where filthy fingernails tear into his flesh.

The assistant ME continues screaming. I smell piss too, but I think that's coming from the doctor.

Before Rambles can rip open his jugular, I bash my forearm into hers, snapping the bones like twigs. The dead woman's grip fails, letting the doctor collapse to the floor. Rambles grabs my hair, using it to pull herself up off the table and go for my face with her teeth.

Sorry, bitch. I'm not into girls.

I pound her in the nose, knocking her flat on the slab hard enough to break open the back of her skull. Focus leaves the woman's eyes. Huh, guess massive brain damage still works on these things… at least for the few seconds it takes them to knit back together. Already, the doctor's incision on her chest has sealed.

"Em… flare time!" I shout while pummeling the dead woman in the jaw, hoping a broken neck keeps her immobilized for a few seconds more.

When I jump back, Emerson shoots a flare into her side. The fizzling projectile embeds itself in her flesh, leaving a one-inch hole spouting smoke. A second later, she's fully engulfed, arms and legs twitching fast enough to blur. Not that there's much in here but concrete, tiles, and steel, but I hold her down with telekinesis anyway. Egg-sized blisters swell up on her skin, rupturing to spit streams of burning undead blood onto the floor that tint the room a sickly yellow-green in the glare.

The assistant ME snaps out of her blind terror and rushes forward to grab the doctor and drag him clear of the burning jets. Ten seconds later, Rambles stops moving. Her corpse blackens and smolders away to a state resembling an ancient mummy.

"You okay, Doc?" asks Emerson.

"He's going to need stitches and a ton of antibiotics," says the assistant while wrapping gauze around his neck. "Come on, Doctor Bearce. We need to go upstairs."

Dazed, the doctor offers a mute nod and stands, allowing the much younger woman to lead him out into the hall.

"Heh. Looks like Doctor Bearce has an appointment with Doctor Jack Daniels in his future."

Emerson shakes his head, fighting the urge to laugh. "That's not funny."

"Now what? We pulling an all-nighter?"

He rubs the bridge of his nose. "This is going to take a little while. Look, we can do the sketch artist thing in the morning. No reason you need to stand around here all night. This is all on video."

"Right. Okay. I can get myself home if you don't need me here."

"Thanks for helping."

I wink. "No problem. See you tomorrow."

"You okay?" He raises both eyebrows. "This isn't like bothering you?"

"Nah. It's kinda funny the way they flail when they're on fire."

He stares.

"What? The woman's already dead." I sigh. Something tells me burning is *less* painful than existing for them.

After assuring Emerson I'm fine, I meander down the hallway, go outside, and walk to a nice, secluded spot where no one can watch my wings come out.

18

POLAR OPPOSITE

I spend a good hour soaking in hot water after flying home. No amount of 'Silken Extravagance' bath bomb is going to erase the memory of smelling whiskey-zombie puke or having a dead man's junk rubbing on my thigh. Burning those pants is still an option. Before crawling into bed around midnight, I send Lieutenant Sims a text.

‹Stayed up late w police investigation. More tomorrow. Page me if there's a fire.›

With that, I pass out and sleep hard—not stirring until eight the next morning.

Skipping lunch and dinner yesterday catches up to me and I overdo breakfast a bit, inhaling two frozen egg burritos. Miraculously, my rune oven doesn't turn them into chocolate marshmallow with sausage and onions like last time.

Lieutenant Sims' text of ‹Okay. Be careful› makes me smile. Pestering Natalie about necromancers probably won't get me anywhere, so I hatch a new plan. Emerson mentioned a Lifemage works for free out of the basilica, but I don't really feel like going to a church. I know myself too well. Not like I'm afraid of the priests or anything, but I will not be able to resist making fun of them. After pulling on a *clean* fire department polo and BDU pants, I send Emerson a text to meet me at Pennsylvania Hospital on Spruce, and head up to the roof.

Wow. I'm getting way casual about flying. Maybe I should dial that back a bit. In the span of a few days, both Lieutenant Sims and Emerson have crept into my 'zone of secrecy.' If things keep going at this rate, I might as well just walk around town in full armor with my wings out. I send him another text asking for a ride, and go back to my apartment. He replies with ‹Okay› twice in a row.

I wait about ten minutes and head downstairs to wait at the front door. Emerson pulls up in the same unmarked silver sedan not too long after, greeting me with a smile as I climb in.

"What's this about the hospital?"

"They have a Lifemage on staff there. I want to talk to them. Maybe they'll be able to tell us something useful, and the odds of them seeing us are a lot better with an 'official police request.' I'm guessing you haven't done that yet."

"No... up until you started helping, I'd been hoping this was a nice normal serial killer."

I laugh.

WITH THE MAGIC OF 'HI I'M A DETECTIVE,' EMERSON GETS US A meeting with Pennsylvania Hospital's Lifemage. Even with it being an 'official' request, we sit close to fifteen minutes in a small but pleasant waiting room with pale blue walls and squarish beige mini sofas.

A platinum blonde woman strolls in wearing a blindingly white garment that's half-wizard's robe and half-doctor's coat. Geez. What the heck is it with mages? At least she's not carrying a quarterstaff. Her outfit has the hospital's logo on the breast. Two gold bands adorn the robe's puffy shoulders, like some kind of military insignia, with matching decoration at the ends of her sleeves. I figure her for around thirty. She's near perfect, which gets me suspicious she might be an Elestari.

That suspicion is fleeting, gone as soon as I read her. She's mostly benevolent, but more than a touch self-important. Guess having people's lives literally in her hands goes to her head.

"Good morning, detective," says the Lifemage, a strong French accent in her voice. "I am Aline Lyon. I understand you 'ave some questions for me?"

"Yes. Thank you for agreeing to see us." Emerson stands and offers a handshake, which the woman accepts with a mild grimace of alarm. "We were hoping you could help us understand some things of a magical nature related to a murder investigation."

Aline gasps. "Oh, my. That is most 'orrible."

I offer a mild bow of greeting, making no move to shake her hand. Not sure if she's a germophobe or simply doesn't want to touch peasants, but I can score some goodwill. "Miss Lyon"—I do my best to pronounce her last name with the right emphasis. Hey anything for brownie points—"I was curious if you could help us understand necromancers... since like they're your direct opposite."

"*Oui.*" She shakes her head with a sad sigh. "Many of my brethren like to perpetuate the lie that we are so different from them. Necromancy is much closer to our magic than most would care to admit. The use of arcane energy to manipulate life, the body... it is like sister and brother. The underlying theory is identical; the only difference—the primary difference—is whether the recipient of the magic is living or deceased. While I've never studied necromantic implementations, the schools are close enough to share some general proficiency. Unlike, say, a Hydromancer attempting fire magic."

I nod, as does Emerson.

"So... would you know how long it normally takes a zombie or a nazedeh to sit up after it's created?" I ask.

"Oh... that much I do know." Aline's grimace returns and her eyes radiate sorrow at the idea of it. "They should show signs of animation right away—as soon as the incantation is complete. But, creating zombies is illegal." She glances at Emerson. "I imagine that is why you are here."

"Yes." Emerson examines his tablet. "We've discovered ten so far."

Aline looks down. "That is most 'orrible. You must put a stop to this awful person."

This woman's almost as nice as my mom. They could be twins. Like, if Mom were the type to shriek and jump on a chair at the sight of a mouse... and happened to be French. Ehh... I'm sure this mage has seen things far more grotesque than a mouse, but someone who's close to tearing up at the idea of a zombie has to be over-sensitive. She probably weeps at intense sunsets too.

"What would it mean if they don't start moving right away? So far, the victims we've seen are getting back up anywhere from about three to ten hours." I explain that I had a vision of the necromancer, and that he seemed enraged after throwing magic into the body.

"Maybe he doesn't even know he's making zombies," says Emerson.

Aline looks up, clasping her hands together at her chest while fixing him with an earnest, worried stare. "*Oui*, umm, yes. I believe you are correct. Especially since he is leaving them to be found. Few practice necromancy openly. There is a man in New York City, I believe in the employ of the medical examiner's office."

"Asking the dead how they died?" I quirk an eyebrow.

She nods.

Oh, that's unsettling. Kinda cool though.

"Right, so we have an accidental necromancer." Emerson frowns. "You said he was young?"

"Twenties probably." I shrug. "Looked pretty clean cut. Wasn't even rocking a robe."

Aline makes a tiny head shake motion. "The man would most likely not wish to draw attention to himself as a mage."

"Thank you." I smile at her and turn to Emerson. "Sounds like the guy is trying to make something bigger than a zombie, and it's not working. What's our next move? Sketch artist?"

"Yep." He bows to Aline. "Thank you for your time, Miss Lyon."

"A pleasure, Detective Zheng. Anything I can do to assist you in stopping a necromancer from killing the innocent."

"Oh, sorry. One more question?" I blurt as she turns to leave.

"They seem quite susceptible to being burned. Is there a less dangerous way to… ease their suffering?"

Aline thinks for a few seconds before eyeing me up and down. "Only if you are a mage. With the nazedeh, I could sever the magic binding their souls to their remains. They would simply fall where they stand. If you are not a Lifemage or a Necromancer, fire is the only practical way."

"Is there an impractical way?" asks Emerson.

"If you are near a volcano, or a pit of acid." Aline's faint Mona Lisa smile gives way to a somber expression. "I truly wish you can stop this man."

Emerson nods at the door. "We're doing everything we can."

"Thanks." I follow him out.

Other than the irritating feeling we should be grateful she deigned to allow us to bask in her presence, she seemed friendly. I wonder how much of that is me. Arrogant people piss me off. Rich people can be okay if they don't treat everyone else like peons. There's an association between Lifemages and arrogance, but I can't say I've ever spoken to one before today. Guess it's like how everyone believes all lawyers are the scum of the earth until they meet a decent one.

Hmm. Maybe demons just need better PR.

19

ENIGMA

W orking with the police sketch artist takes about an hour, after which we've got a pretty decent rendition of the guy I saw. Emerson cuts me loose for the time being, since he doesn't need 'psychic help' tracking down a guy based on a picture. I head to the fire station and check in with Sims. After giving him a rundown of the case and what I've been doing with the time he's let me take, it's back to fire engines for me.

I wind up helping Herlihy rebuild the pump on our secondary truck. Since I'm no mechanic, my 'helping' consists mostly of giving him a hand lifting and moving heavy stuff, or passing him tools. Brian does take the time to explain shit to me, so maybe I'll eventually be able to do this myself. He replaces some bushings and one impeller, but otherwise we mostly just clean the damn thing.

He gives me a raised eyebrow when I heft the upper half of the outer shell back into place myself.

"What?" I ask.

"That thing's almost 200 pounds." He hands me some bolts.

"I'm telekinetic. And no, I didn't use it when I threw Lamar arm wrestling. He's just weak." I wink.

"Ahh." Herlihy laughs. "Telekinetic, huh? Move stuff wit' yer mind?"

"Yep."

He makes an impressed frown, nods, and proceeds to replace bolts on the left while I do the right side.

Jason swoops in a few minutes before six, when I'm sitting in the barracks reading the driver's license book for the ninth time. "Hey... you busy tonight?"

Damn. I toss the book to the bed and stand into a hug. "Had plans with Natalie... girls' night out. I can ask her if she'd mind if you come along?"

"It's okay." He winks. "I have a PlayStation. Tomorrow?"

"Absolutely." I kiss him. "Hey. We're the only ones in the barracks. Quickie?"

His face goes as red as his beard.

"Oh, come on. Live a little." I look around like I'm checking for witnesses before breaking into the mall again. Okay, open bunks maybe a bit *too* much for him. "Here."

I lead him to a storage closet. He's nervous as hell, and it takes him a while to get it up, but eventually our heavy make-out session advances to full on lovemaking. Slightly bent forward, my pants around my knees, I hang on to the shelves while he enters me from behind. I'm not at all into kink, but he clamps his hand over my mouth as a gag, purely so we don't get caught. Apparently, I'm vocal. His other hand slides up under my shirt, rubbing my breasts as we hit the same rhythm. I try my best not to squeal with each thrust, but without his hand being over my mouth, we'd be *so* busted. I float in a sea of pleasure for a few minutes before Jason shudders with release. Feeding from the psychic energy he throws off at that instant is enough (on top of the thrill of breaking the rules) to set off my bomb too. We keep going for a little while more before he withdraws, and we turn to face each other.

Crap. Rolled those dice again. I glance down and do a double take when I notice he'd gotten a condom on. Wow, he's like a prophylactic ninja; I never even noticed him do that. That gets me giggling, which is probably not the best thing to do when staring at a guy's sword.

Jason fidgets.

"Oh. No… not that." I caress it while kissing him. "Didn't realize you had a raincoat on."

"Fastest packet in the west." He winks.

It's a total lie though. I'm like his third girlfriend and only the second one he's gone all the way with. "We should get out of here."

"Yeah."

We fix our clothes back in place. The barracks sound clear, so I risk opening the door. I expect to find a line of guys clapping, but we're still alone. Whew. I stagger out into the open and slouch with relief. Guess after a couple zombies and being told millennia-old creatures made me to destroy the world, I *can* catch a little break.

"I'll call you when I get home."

He kisses me again. "Okay."

I hurry to the showers for a quick clean up.

When I arrive home, I find Ashley and Tracy standing outside my door. Tracy rings the bell. Ashley spots me coming down the corridor and points at me while tugging on her mother's arm.

"What's up?" I ask when I come to a stop beside them.

Tracy spins toward me, a mix of confusion and desperation in her eyes. "Can Ash please stay with you for a little bit tonight? I got a class. I was about to take her with me, but I don't know if the school would let her in."

Hell with it. Girls' night out, right? She's a girl. "I had dinner plans with a friend, but if you're okay with me taking Ashley out to eat, no problem."

"Oh, umm." Tracy looks down.

"I'm not expecting you to pay for her. I wouldn't offer if I wasn't planning to cover it." Except for fast food, I don't think I went out to eat until I'd been in college.

Tracy stands there in silence, tears rolling down her cheeks.

"You're doing okay." I pat the woman on the shoulder. "When I was

Ashley's age, I didn't even own shoes." And I walked four miles uphill both ways to class. "Go on. Do the school thing."

"Thank you," croaks Tracy.

Ashley hugs her mother. After the obligatory 'be good and don't cause trouble' admonitions, Tracy hurries off to the stairwell. The kid's in a plain white dress with thin band of pink trim around the neckline and sleeves. It's got a few smudges, but it doesn't look like she crawled out of a war zone. Her sneakers are a little battered, but the frilled pink socks add a nice touch. Not like Natalie and I are going to an expensive joint, so I doubt anyone will bat an eye at her.

She follows me inside and occupies herself with the PlayStation while I change. The closet sex still has me fired up in a wild mood, so I pull on a black brocade top with lacy cuffs and one of my 'faux-tattered' black skirts. The fishnet vs solid black leggings argument kills a few minutes, but I wind up going with black. Only my being too lazy to clean it off later prevents me from adding heavy black eye shadow. I content myself with black lip-gloss and again grumble mentally about the department's nail polish rule.

Natalie's ‹I'm here› text makes my cell tweep soon after I start co-opping the jelly game with Ash.

"Ready to eat?"

Ashley nods. "Yeah. I'm starving."

"What'd you have today?"

She looks down. "Egg muffin this morning and toast for lunch."

"Toast?"

"Yeah, with jam. It's not mommy's fault. She doesn't get much money."

"Once when I was nine, my mother's car had a problem. She had to get it fixed. I went like a week eating saltines." Plus whatever I could shoplift. The not having shoes thing was creative license to make Tracy feel better. Mom did take care of me. Getting stuck eating Saltines for a week actually happened, and that was the pair of us. Mom too. It's not like she made me eat crackers while she had real food. I *still* can't stand them.

Ashley sticks her tongue out. "Bleh."

I laugh. "Yeah, they tasted like cardboard."

She holds my hand and we go downstairs to meet Natalie and her cute little car with the blinking fake eyelashes on the headlights out front. Seeing Ashley surprises her, but she keeps right on smiling. A few minutes into the ride, Natalie spins around in the middle of driving and starts asking the kid how her day went.

Ashley screams, pointing at the windshield.

"Oh, it's fine. She's driving herself." Natalie winks.

"Hah! I knew it." I poke Nat in the side.

Ashley had a super-exciting day of playing with stuffed animals and flicking paint flakes across her bedroom. Ugh. At least I grew up kinda out in the sticks where I could run around trees and visit a small lake next to the trailer park. Our neighborhood's not the safest place for a small girl to roam alone outside.

We arrive at the steakhouse I picked after a twenty-minute ride. I'd wanted to go to that Portuguese place, but turns out they seat by reservation only, and they had no openings tonight. So, I chose safe—one of those chain restaurants that claims to have roots in Texas, but are as genuinely country as almond milk comes from cows. While we're waiting for our table-pager to go off, an already-mostly-drunk guy in a cowboy hat, mirrored sunglasses, and a grey shirt overhanging his belt hits on Natalie. The buttons on that belly are going to fly off with little blue spirals trailing them like a railgun, any second now.

I'm not sure what annoys me more, that the guy's clearly around fifty and he's hitting on Nat, or that he thinks I'm the 'younger sister.' Even without my gift, I can tell he's got no interest beyond one night. My brain cooks up a line about calling Natalie 'mom' and asking her if she thinks this guy could handle both of us at once... but as funny as it would be to see his face, Natalie would kill me and Ashley's right here.

Instead, I take the high road. "No thanks, dude. You're like old enough to be her father. And your breath could peel paint."

He looks at me for a moment, swaying on his feet, but decides to wander off, muttering about lesbians.

Oh, look at that. Drunk guy 'tripped' over his own feet and went face first into the floor.

Ashley giggles.

A host runs over to 'check on us' and see if we're okay. Natalie brushes it off as no big deal. Oh, and get a load of this… the chair the guy goes to sit in slides out from under him all on its own. At that moment, our pager goes off.

"Table!" I hold up the flashing device.

Leaving the host to ponder tossing the guy out for being too drunk, we head to a nice, quiet booth in the back. This is one of those places where the wait staff makes a giant, embarrassing deal about birthdays. I'm half-tempted to lie and say it's my birthday just to make Natalie turn crimson from embarrassment when everyone in here stares at me being a jackass. So what if I'm twenty-three? I can do the saddle-on-a-stand thing.

We munch on the complimentary bread and order drinks. No sense wasting money. I am *not* dropping $90 on booze in order to notice a buzz, so I get an iced tea. Ashley asks for water, but guiltily switches it to an iced tea too when I press if she really wants water.

A moment after the waitress walks off, Ashley looks down at her lap. She's throwing off more guilt than Santana did the night of the fire. Uh oh.

I brush her hair away from her face and pull her into a one-armed hug. "You okay?"

"I'm sorry for getting in the way."

"You're not in the way." I pat and rub her back. "It's girls' night out."

She looks up, hopeful, but not quite smiling.

"You're a girl, right?"

Ashley nods.

"Then, you're good." I wink and poke her in the belly. "Stop being glum."

"This man said you were gonna hurt me, but I don't believe him." Ashley scowls. "I didn't like the way he looked at me."

Ugh. Not again. "Like Frank?"

She shakes her head. "No. Like he hated I was poor and thought I was dirty."

Oh. Or an Elestari staring down their nose at a human. "Don't listen to him."

"I didn't." She grins. "He looked like an asshole."

A woman at the table across the aisle from us coughs on her drink. Natalie cracks up with a giggle fit too powerful to talk over.

"Ash, those kinds of words aren't for little kids, okay?" When did I turn into my mother? "Save it 'til you're at least fourteen."

"Sorry." She smiles.

"How's it going with Jason?" asks Natalie.

I grin. "Good. Really good, actually."

"Cool." Natalie smiles. Fortunately, she's not jealous. She's in no hurry to do anything but run her enchanting shop. "If I ever meet a guy who's not double my age, I may ask you to give him the ol' sniff."

Ashley tilts her head.

"Brook's good at feeling people out." Natalie winks.

"Oh." Ashley leans close and whispers, "If mommy gets another boyfriend, will you sniff him too?"

"You bet." I pat her on the head.

"And if he's bad, throw him out the window." Ashley nods.

The woman across the aisle glances over at us. I lock stares with her and *really* want her to mind her own damn business. Her eyes flutter and she goes back to her meal. Heh. This is kinda cool.

"Oh. Before I forget… here." Natalie pulls something out of her purse and reaches across the table, dangling a one-inch tall diamond-shaped gold amulet on a length of jeweler's chain.

"Oh, Nat…" I cradle the pendant, which has a bas-relief of a chibi succubus. "That's adorable."

She grins. "Oh, it's not a big deal. Minor enchantment. If you're wearing it and rub the pendant, it'll create an illusion of clothing around your body."

"What kind of clothing?"

Natalie gestures at me. "Pretty much like what you usually wear, Doom Queen." She winks.

I give her a playful raspberry and put it on. "Thank you."

Our food arrives. Ashley got breaded chicken strips with fries, while Natalie and I both did the steak thing. The provided knives are on the dull side. Sigh. Are they really worried about random patron violence that they can't give us better than this serrated quasi-sharp bullshit?

Natalie saws at her sirloin, making a face. "Wow, the meat's not tough at all but these knives…"

"Hmm." I look around to make sure no one's watching and push my panties down enough so I can let the tail out without shredding them. Careful to be subtle, I serpent it up over the table edge and grab the end near the long onyx blade at the tip. Ashley and Natalie stare at me as I wield it like a knife, slicing the steak with ease. "What?"

"Umm," whispers Natalie. "You don't know where that's been. I mean… You *do* know where that's been. Under your skirt."

Ashley keeps staring at the blade, but her expression is well into 'wow, that's cool' territory.

"It turns into smoke when I put it away. It's clean." I finish cutting my dinner and hold it up. "Wanna borrow it?"

Curiosity gets the better of her after a few seconds, and she nods. I pull my tail back under the table and thread it across to the other side so she can grab it. It's long enough to reach without me scooting forward. She studies the maybe fourteen-inch blade at the end with awe. Once she finally stops gawking, the edge makes short work of her steak. As soon as she's done, I 'put it away,' and it dissipates into a whorl of dark vapors right in her hand.

"Whoa, that's awesome," says Ashley.

"Holy shit, Brook… it cut the plate too."

"Not all the way through I hope."

She shakes her head. "That's a heck of a weapon."

I murmur a hair over a whisper about the golem fight, enthralling Natalie like a little kid at a campfire ghost story. From there, our conversation goes off in random directions, and for a little while, it's easy to forget all about zombies, serial killers, and assholes with huge golden wings.

WE DECIDE TO DO A MOVIE (AT HOME) AFTER DINNER, AND ROLL THE scary dice of letting Ashley choose what to watch. Natalie pulls into an open parking spot about a block from my building. On the walk back, two guys and a woman step out of the shadows across the street near where I put a beer bottle through the window of a car a couple days ago. They're all in jeans and leather jackets, and have this air about them that gives me the impression they're intending to pick a fight.

Worse, I can't read anything off them. Fuck.

They step onto the sidewalk in front of us.

Ashley clamps onto me from behind, trembling. Natalie's crystal earrings glow amber, projecting arcs of luminous writing in strange symbols around her head.

The hell? No time to grill her over magic right now. I smirk at the three. "The Hells Angels gathering's not for another few months... or are you guys looking for the kink bar? That's two blocks over."

"Cute," says the wider of the two men. He's almost a caricature of humanity. Massive shoulders and chest, but his legs are so tiny, it's laughable.

"Dude. You gotta work on your human suit. You look like a cartoon... a meatball on toothpicks. Is your d—" I cringe and glance at Ashley out of the corner of my eye. "Hope everything isn't that tiny."

His face reddens.

"You can say 'dick.'" Ashley rolls her eyes. "That's not a bad word."

"So insouciant," says the woman. She's an inch taller than me, long black hair, and a thick, muscular build. "I love it. Shame we gotta do this."

"I think that was a bad word," says Ashley.

The third man's more reasonable in size, but he's still over six feet and built like a pro wrestler. He also went for a Hispanic look, probably trying to blend in around here. "Ain't personal."

"Whoa." I hold up a 'wait a second' finger before peeling Ashley away and handing her to Natalie. "There's an epic amount of bullshit flying around these days. Which particular nugget of misinformation are you three munching on?"

Meatball's expression becomes constipated. A few seconds later, his chest shrinks while his legs grow, evening out his size distribution.

"Better." I golf clap. "The knuckle-dragging mouthbreather thing wasn't working for you."

"What's going on?" whispers Natalie. "Something tried to affect my mind."

"I think these three are trying to get me to buy demon scout cookies. Might wanna take Ashley and back up a bit."

The woman snickers. "Oh, man. I like her."

"It's been decided that your existence is too much of a risk. You are too unsafe to remain alive, an unexpected enigma," says the Hispanic impersonator.

"Oh, *that* particular wafer of bull. I'm not going to break the Armistice. How many times do I have to say it?"

"Your intentions are admirable, but we would rather not take the chance," says Meatball.

Natalie barks, *"Inzhor borel."*

A flash of blue-white light behind me accompanies a startled yelp from Ashley.

The eyes of all three Shaar'Nath glow blue.

Dammit. I like this outfit. This is one of my prettier tops.

The instant I spot claws growing out of their hands, I hurl myself into a full shift. The ground falls downward as my height springs up to about seven feet. My clothes all seem to have vanished entirely, though the white armor plating of my present form doesn't feel 'naked.' Ashley's awestruck gasp follows the leathery ruffle of my wings appearing.

All three of them shift as well. Meatball's armor plating is jet-black, and he's goddamned massive. I feel like a twelve-year-old staring up at a pissed off cop... with wings, horns, and a bladed tail. The other guy's only a head taller than me, and dark crimson, while the woman's got me by three inches or so. Her armor's a dark charcoal grey.

I'm outnumbered, so I decide to go aggressive. Batshit crazy often makes up for even a big disadvantage. While pummeling the woman with the same telekinetic *away* I used to throw that one punk out of Kwan's market and into a bus, I dive left at the crimson-plated Shaar'Nath.

The woman flies straight backward, landing atop a parked car and smashing the roof in, the windows exploding in a blast of flickering bits of sparkle. My sudden attack catches Crimson off guard and my right hand claws leave four nice gouges down his chest, dribbling with black blood. He grabs for my throat, but I leap to the side and spin around, trying to get behind him. A shimmering column of blue catches my eye next to Natalie.

Ashley's standing inside a box of light that's only an inch or so taller than her, pounding on the side like she's trapped within a phone booth of glass. Her mouth's wide open, but I can't hear any screaming.

Meatball pounces and grabs my left wing, hauling me off my feet by it while he swings me around. Before he can let go and send me face-first into the wall, I whip my tail up and slice his left hand off at the wrist. He roars in pain and loses his hold, causing me to career toward the street instead. Black blood and sparkly peach-colored energy spray out of the stump.

I catch myself in midair, hovering.

The car creaks and groans as the female Shaar'Nath pulls herself out of it.

Natalie yells something unintelligible and a weird tingle spreads over me.

"You three are making a mistake," I say. "I want the same thing you do. I mean… I don't want me dead. I want the Armistice to remain."

Crimson mutters in another language, but I'm sure he called me something unpleasant. He leaps into a flying charge, raising his claws, but I see the fake-out coming. Flinging myself to the right and down, I catch his bladed tail slashing for my throat while twisting under his distracting claws. My tail whips around in an arc and takes his head clean off. I finish my spin by ramming the business end of *his* tail into his heart.

Ashley screams.

Unfortunately, as flashy as that was, I've trapped myself against him with his tail around my back. His weight pulls me to the ground, fortunately with me on top. Before I can wrench the eighteen-inch onyx blade out of his armored chestplate, his body glows and disintegrates into a cloud of peach-hued light.

Damn. Eighteen inches… his was bigger than mine.

Free, I bounce to my feet and face the other two, claws poised.

They've stopped a short distance away, hesitating. Meatball looks concerned. The woman has less (though still some) fear in her eyes, but flares her wings in a challenging display.

"You're only sending us back home," sneers the woman.

"Maybe the fiftieth time you guys try, I might have to actually work for it." I wink.

She growls, but doesn't advance. "We won't let you break the Armistice. You can't kill us."

"Perhaps *she* cannot." Dad appears out of thin air beside me, still in his nice suit, his hair perfect, his half-smile unflappable. "But *I* can."

Did I mention I have the most interesting dad in the world?

"Dad…" I fake whine while gesturing at them with my claws. "I had this."

Both Meatball and the woman step back, bowing their heads.

"Do not harm my daughter."

Meatball bows deep. "Baal'nethiel, you must understand the risk."

"You fail to grasp the risk involved with crossing me," says Dad, as calm as if deciding against buying a car.

Meatball straightens. Fear and frustration collide with visible shaking. "But, the Armistice…"

"She could be controlled, as her mother was. *Made* to do their bidding." The woman flicks her claws at me. "She has enough human to be susceptible."

"And enough Shaar'Nath to be immune," says Dad. "The lot of you are fools for believing that line of drivel. Falsehoods stirred by the warmongers. Are you so quick to condemn our kind to annihilation?"

"You believe we would lose?" asks the woman.

Dad examines his fingernails. "Impulse and savagery will not compare to calculated hatred. By the time our brethren took the war to heart, we would already be lost."

"I do not wish for war, but I believe you fail to give our kind due respect." The woman squeezes her hands into fists, not quite making eye contact with my father.

"It was decided that she risks the Armistice." Meatball's voice comes off halting, like he's trying to suggest a reasonable plan to a crazy evil mastermind, and expecting to be shot for it.

"Neither my daughter nor I will allow that to come to pass." Dad smiles at me with pride, though I think he just told them he'll kill me himself if he has to.

The woman bows at him and fades away.

Once Meatball disappears, I relax and shift back to human. When my clothing reappears intact, I let out a squeak of surprise and pat myself down. Whoa. Really here... not illusions.

Natalie edges up behind me and whispers, "Umm. Who is *that?*"

"Cool your hormones. That's my father." I glance back at Ashley, still beating on the inside of her energy cage. "What did you do to Ash?"

"It's a shield. A semi-truck could run into that at full speed and she'd be fine."

My eyebrows go up. "Wow. Nice. She looks kinda trapped though."

"Oh, yeah." Natalie nods. "That spell gains defensive power by exchanging the inability to do anything while you're in it. Really, it's meant for noncoms."

"What?"

"Noncombatants," says Dad. "The man who devised that enchant a few centuries ago made it for his wife."

"Can you let her out before she's scarred for life?" I ask, while hurrying over to Ashley.

"Yeah sure." Natalie gazes into space for a moment, and the barrier drops.

Ashley leaps into my arms. Sniveling and shaking lasts only

seconds before she goes platter-eyed. "That was *so* cool! You kicked their ass! Why'd Miss Diaz put me in a box?"

"So you didn't get hurt," says Natalie.

"I'm not a hamster." Ashley sticks out her tongue.

Natalie grasps the child's head and tilts her so she looks at the crushed car. "I didn't want one of them landing on you."

"Eep!" yells Ashley.

"Nat, am I wearing illusions now? They feel solid."

She grins. "They are solid. If you've got that amulet on when you change shape, it'll 'eat' your clothes and hold them until you change back. If something happens that shreds your outfit, you can rub the amulet and it'll make an illusion of clothing."

"Awesome. Umm, Dad?" Cradling Ashley still, I pivot to face him. "Those three were full Shaar'Nath, right?"

"They were." He nods once.

"Umm. Why… how… I mean… I'm confused."

"Evidently." Dad smiles.

"How did I kill him so fast? Or… sent him away, or whatever I did? Aren't they like way more powerful than me 'cause they're pure-blooded?"

Dad shakes his head. "Your combined heritage gives you a strong advantage here in the Armistice. From your mother, your human side brings with it traces of the Elestari, the magic they poured into creating this world. None of our kind are certain exactly what you are capable of. Were you in Imbreleth, I imagine those three would've been somewhat more potent than you, but I do not think it would be a great difference." His eyes flare with inspiration. "If any. Some alloys are significantly stronger than any of their base components."

"What about the other place?" I fidget. "Not that I ever want to go there, but…"

"Aesinor?" Dad's expression becomes the most clueless I've ever seen him. "I have only read tales of the time before the Armistice, when our kind could cross freely into their realm. Both they and us draw power from the realms in which we reside. The Shaar'Nath overwhelm the Elestari in Imbreleth, the reverse is true in Aesinor. I do not know exactly how you would fare in the realm of light, but I encourage you never to find out."

"Yeah. If I have anything to say about it, I never plan to." I squeeze Ashley, pat her on the back twice, and set her on her feet. "Ugh. So now I have to look over my shoulder for our kind too?"

"Alas." Dad sighs. "Those who crave war may or may not call for your blood if they believe you shall not do their bidding."

"But the pacifists want to kill her," says Natalie. "That's pretty twisted."

I gaze down at my hands, my impossibly white skin stained with black blood. "Kill one me to prevent billions of deaths. It makes sense."

Ashley grabs my hand and stares defiance up at Dad. "They can't have her. She's *my* demon. I still need her."

I can't help but laugh.

20

OLD FAMILY SECRET

few hours of digital animation helps me deal with the worry of my existence. At least I'm not 'prophesied to save the world' or something. I'm expected to destroy it. Though, being a slacker at heart, it's awesome that my best option is to do nothing. I don't have to dread dragging myself to the ends of the Earth and busting my ass on some one-in-a-thousand chance task. Nope. All I need to do to save the world is plant my ass on my couch.

After Ashley returns home with her mother, Nat puts on a creepy movie about some cabin off in the middle of nowhere and paranormal shit going on, but we don't pay much attention to it. I wind up full shifting and standing there while my friend studies me like I'm some statue in a long-abandoned temple. The last half of the movie passes in relative normality with us flopped on the sofa.

Once Natalie goes home for the night, I call Jason and let the conversation go wherever it goes. He keeps trying to tell me how awesome I am, which gets me to redirect elsewhere. I don't mind him saying how I make him feel, but I can do without the worship. When I finally fall asleep, my brain rebounds from responsibility and goes back to the moment I felt the most free in my life: six-year-old me eluding Mrs. Martinez (a sweet old woman who wound up being the trailer park's version of daycare) and going for a walkabout in my birthday suit. About half the residents thought me cute, a few yelled, and one or two tried to catch me so they could drag me back home. I wound up playing in the creek that fed the nearby lake for a while before hunger sent me home.

Mom wasn't too happy with me, but that day... hours to myself, innocent with nothing to worry about... sigh. Overall, being a kid and having no freedom *did* suck, but moments like that I could seriously go back to.

Adulting blows.

So does waking up at 5:00 a.m. I have a normal morning, other than my reluctant departure from bed delaying breakfast until I run to the Starbucks for the fire station crew. Maybe I shouldn't have told Herlihy I'm telekinetic, because all the guys keep goading me into demonstrations. Lieutenant Sims walks in while I'm making a spare hose behave like a cobra. He takes one look and stops dead in his tracks, blinks, and backs out without saying a thing.

The guys erupt in laughter.

A couple minutes before eleven, we get a call to a residence a few blocks from the station house for a 'minor incident.' Five of us hop on a truck and roll. I'm expecting a kitchen grease fire or something along those lines.

What I'm not expecting is a severely obese man who accidentally sat on his toilet with the seat up, and got stuck. His wife is verging on a panic attack while his two tween sons are crying from laughing so hard. The kids cackle even louder when O'Keefe sincerely asks Humberto if he should get the Jaws of Life.

"I got it," I mutter, and follow the wife upstairs to the master bath.

A glum-faced guy in his late thirties in a nauseatingly yellow polo shirt sits on the bowl. Other than miserable, he looks unhurt. Seems like his generous backside has made a total seal and he can't get up.

Four or five years ago, I wouldn't have been able to look at this scene without joining the guy's sons laughing my ass off. I'm far more mature now. A giant shit-eating grin isn't exactly professional though.

"It's gonna be okay, sir." I crouch nearby. "Pardon me." One hand on his leg, I push a curtain of flesh up from obscuring the interface point where porcelain meets skin.

The guy's face reddens. I bite back the 'maybe he'll leave the seat down now' comment, and focus on a telekinetic prod, creating a gap between him and the bowl so air can flow. He must feel the suction release, as he grabs at the sink and wall for support and lifts himself up.

I turn away the instant I no longer need to concentrate on breaking the seal, to give him privacy.

"Oh my, Harold…" The wife hovers at the door. She rushes in as soon as I'm out of the way.

An EMT who'd been waiting in the hallway steps in to check the man over. My part done, I head downstairs. On the way back to the station, the guys share stories of some of the weirder calls they've been on that didn't involve fire, and we come to the conclusion that whenever the cops or the EMTs have no idea what the hell to do with a situation, they call us.

After we put our gear away, I borrow one of the computers in the lounge and make an appointment with a driving school. Figure it can't hurt to get some practice. The day progresses in a blur of ping-pong and sitting around watching television. Sims causes a mix of groans and whoops when he announces we're all due for a refresher on the high-rise fire simulation course.

At least that won't be boring.

Tires squeal outside a few minutes past two.

Sims' voice comes over the PA soon after. "Brooklyn, that detective's here for you."

The guys tease me a little about 'playing for the other team' as I get up to leave.

"What'll Dunn say?" asks Humberto.

Jason grins.

"Well, I suppose he'll just have to suffer a threesome if I can ever find a woman good enough to share him with." I wink at Jason—hopefully he knows I'm completely teasing—and duck out of the lounge.

Laughter chases me down the hall, and I think someone slugs him in the shoulder while calling him a lucky bastard.

Emerson's still in the car, passenger door open. Uh oh, this looks serious. I sprint across the garage and jump in.

"What's up?"

He pulls out into traffic, lights and siren going. "The necromancer attacked another victim, but we had a good Samaritan this time. Someone shot the guy and chased him off before he could finish whatever magic bullshit he's doing."

"Okay."

We're quiet for the rest of a maybe nine-minute ride before an ocean of flashing police lights up ahead make the street glow. Emerson stops hard, kills the engine, and badges us past the outer perimeter. I keep my mouth shut and follow while trying to convey as much of an 'I'm supposed to be here' attitude as I can.

The body of a homeless man lays sprawled against a dumpster, like he'd been trying to scramble upright when the necromancer shot him. Blood's soaked the front of an olive drab shirt, and his green camo fatigue pants are ripped in multiple places. Only socks cover his feet, somewhat. Weathered toes jut out the tips like eagle's talons. Looks like he absorbed a single bullet to the chest. Damn. Poor guy.

A cluster of patrol officers hover around while some people in blue jumpsuits with 'forensics' in all caps across their backs comb the alley.

"What've we got?" asks Emerson.

"Well…" A black woman with sergeant's stripes approaches, shaking her head. "The few who stuck around when we showed up told us this guy's been a fixture of the area for years. Only knew him by the name Calvin. Got two shooters. Found .45 brass here, two 9mm casings out on the sidewalk. Some gangbanger decided to play cowboy, but he took off before we got here."

No shit. "You guys would've busted him for an illegal weapon, right?"

The sergeant, and some of the other cops around us shrug at me.

"Two witnesses saw it go down," says the sergeant. "Mr. Khan in the restaurant over there, and a patron at a window table. White male, early thirties, 'expensive' coat. Walks into the alley and opens fire on Calvin. Couple local 'bad boys' were hanging out by the 7-Eleven over there. One of 'em comes runnin' and lets Mr. Slick have it. Then, both get the hell outta Dodge. Guy who killed Calvin didn't fire back at the punk, just ran off."

I perk up. "Was the killer hit?"

She shrugs and gestures at the forensics people. "You'll haveta ask those guys."

While Emerson runs over the witness statements with the patrol cops, I wander the area, looking around. They've got a little yellow sign standing on the alley next to a spent shell casing. It's probably the one the necromancer used. I doubt they'll let me touch it, so I don't even ask. Emerson hasn't mentioned anything about the sketch artist's composite, so I'm guessing it hasn't led them to anyone yet.

The cops rehash with Emerson what the restaurant owner said, that the gangbanger opened fire on the killer when he'd knelt over the body. I chuckle to myself when the cops claim being baffled why someone would rob a homeless man. That's not why our guy crouched over the body. With any luck, getting shot at interrupted him before he turned Calvin into a nazedeh.

I circle back near the dead guy and spot a trail of blood dribbles leading off to the street. Score! A tall man in a forensics jumpsuit looks over and down at me when I touch two fingers to the largest puddle. He's got a startlingly large nose, long black hair, and his face tapers to a narrow chin. According to the badge clipped to his chest, he's Kyle Larson.

"Fire department?" asks Kyle with a note of incredulity. "What are you guys doing here?"

"I'm helping Detective Zheng out. Special consultant." I bring my hand up and stare at the blood coating my fingertips.

"Why are you touching my crime scene?"

"Trying to find this guy before he kills someone else. Don't you have a galaxy far, far away to go subjugate or something?"

He squints at me. "We can't have you contaminating the scene."

Ignoring him, I focus on the red spots. A wash of amber light dances over them and I hurtle my thoughts through the tiny doorway. Gotcha. The glow startles the forensics douche into silence. He backs up as I stand, and keeps staring at me while I walk over to Emerson.

"… not being cooperative at all. Won't tell us the name of the guy who tried to help Calvin."

"Detective Zheng." I hold up my fingers. "Sorry to interrupt, but I can find the killer."

"Is that…?" asks Emerson.

"Yes. The gangbanger got a piece of him. The pull isn't going to the dead man."

Emerson grins at me. For a moment, he seems about to kiss me, but instead, he waves one of the patrol officers over. "Grab your partner and follow me. We got a lead on the shooter."

Ugh. Driving. This would be way easier on the wing, but… mage. Yeah. I don't want to do this alone.

21

OVERWHELMING EVIDENCE

My focus on the blood leads us to Bala Cynwyd, a pleasant suburban area northwest of the city center. So many trees here, wow. Somewhat unnerving is the presence of a large cemetery not far away to the east. I never really pictured a necromancer as the quiet suburbanite type, but maybe he made an exception for the convenience of spare parts nearby. Then again, I keep making fun of mages for their bastard hybrids of robes and clothing. S'pose expecting all necromancers to live in caves or dark towers is a bit hypocritical of me.

I give nothing in particular a raspberry, which startles Emerson.

"Bad news?"

"No, just making fun of myself for being surprised a necromancer's living around here and not off in some scary haunted house or something."

A pack of twelve-to-thirteen year old kids go by on bikes, giving the marked car that followed us here a curious look. While radio chatter discusses jurisdictional bullshit, we glide past well-manicured lawns and a woman in a tracksuit walking a flock of tiny dogs.

Emerson clicks on the mic and reads off the address on Trevor Lane. "We're going in. If the locals want to send over a unit, that's fine.

The more the merrier." He lets off the talk button and glances over at me. "Normally, I'd ask you to sit in the car, but you're probably better equipped to deal with this sorta thing than me. Up to you."

He's probably right, though I'd much rather face off against another pyromancer. Something tells me a necromancer's going to be a lot worse. "I'm already here. Might as well."

"Thanks." He taps the address in on the computer. A driver's license photo comes up, but it's not the same guy I saw. He seems about the same age, but this man has a wider jaw with more of a square to his face, and darker hair. "Hmm. Dennis Briggs. Doesn't look much like the sketch."

"No. This isn't the guy I saw in the vision."

Emerson points to a section in the record. "Check this out. He's a registered Lifemage, but a junior one. Still holds the rank of Novice. He's in residence at Temple."

"You think?" I shift my gaze off the screen to lock eyes with Emerson. "Lifemages and Necromancers are pretty close according to that woman we spoke with. And our killer didn't seem to know his pets were getting back up."

"Ugh." Emerson grabs some flare shells from the box between us and stuffs them in his pocket. "We still have three of them out there."

"We can round them up later. Let's stop the source first."

"Agreed… *if* this is the guy."

We get out at the same time. The patrol officers follow suit, and accompany us up to the door, where Emerson rings the bell.

"What? No stomping it in?" I ask.

"Don't have an arrest warrant or probable cause at this point. If the guy at least matched the sketch, maybe… but right now, I'm still in investigation mode."

"Right," I mutter.

The door opens to reveal Dennis Briggs, much the same as his license photo, an upper middle class late-twenties white dude with nothing to worry about. Check that. Who *thinks* he has nothing to worry about. As soon as I lay eyes on him, I know he's the person I've got a blood scent on.

"Can I help you, officers?" asks Briggs.

"Good afternoon." Emerson shows his badge and introduces himself. "I'd like to ask you a few questions about your whereabouts earlier today."

Briggs' smile remains placid. "I've been home all day. My hours at the hospital are mostly weekend. In Friday, home on Monday."

"You're a Lifemage, is that correct?" Emerson glances at me.

"Yes." Briggs nods. "Did you have a medical issue? Normally, these things go through Temple, but I wouldn't mind helping if you want to skip the red tape."

I hold up my fingers. "It's him."

The mage raises an eyebrow at me.

"Mr. Briggs," asks Emerson. "Perhaps you could shed some light on how your blood wound up in downtown Philadelphia near where a man was shot."

"I wouldn't know. Perhaps someone is attempting to misdirect your investigation." Briggs' pleasant smile never wavers.

His demeanor isn't fooling me though. Intent to deceive shines off him like a lighthouse. "He's full of shit." I pause. "Oops. Sorry, guess that's not 'official' sounding. I mean, he's being deceitful. Of course. No wonder he's not injured. *Lifemage.* He already repaired his injuries."

"You must be mistaken, miss," says Briggs.

"I'm not mistaken. I'm psychic."

Emerson reacts to the change in Briggs' posture, tensing up. "A psychic hit isn't enough on its own to make an arrest, but it will be enough for a search warrant."

Oh sure it will. As soon as the judge realizes it's *me* with my juvenile record, he'll laugh Emerson straight out of his office. Or maybe not. I thought juvie records are sealed, though can't exactly seal the judge's memory if he met me before.

"You sure this is the one, detective?" asks one of the patrol officers. "This guy doesn't look like that sketch you sent out."

Briggs grins. "I'm sure there's a reasonable explanation. Obviously, someone is trying to misdirect you."

"Duh." I stare at Emerson, feeling like an idiot. "He's a Lifemage. He can change his face like a mask whenever he goes hunting... and that spike of fear he just gave off tells me I'm right."

"We still need a warrant," mumbles Emerson.

"*Az'ainen L'or.*" Briggs tilts both his hands up like a priest welcoming his sheep.

A rush of whitish-gold light shines away from him, making me numb from head to toe. Emerson and I collapse to the ground together, and a pair of thumps from the grass come from the two patrol officers.

Fuck! I growl in my head, but my body refuses to move at all. I can't even shift.

Briggs plucks the handcuffs from Emerson's belt and locks his hands behind him while muttering. "Do not worry. Your lives are in no danger. My work is meant to *save* people. Besides, killing a police officer never ends well for anyone. No, you will merely forget the past... oh, three or four months."

No... no... no... I keep straining to move, but my eyes won't blink. Three or four *months!?* I'd lose knowing what I am... I'd be defenseless if the Elestari or Shaar'Nath pull more bullshit. And I wouldn't remember Ashley and her mother... Tracy'd ask me for help and I'd think she was still a bitch and bite her head off. Argh! All I can do is stare at the floorboards against my cheek as Brigs steps over me and goes outside. Arcane mutterings precede some grunts, and a moment later, the *clump* of a car door slamming. Emerson's breathing continues at a slow, regular pace, though the panic he's giving off is only a little stronger than mine.

Briggs returns after an eternity of a few minutes and drags us fully inside before closing the door. "Well, miss, you get to go first as your friend here has only one pair of manacles."

The Lifemage scoops me up in his arms. My head lolls back limp, giving me a shitty view of the wall gliding by as he walks. At least he's nice enough not to whack my head on the doorjamb on the way down the basement stairs.

Shit!

Screams and roars in my head aren't helping. Whatever he did to me is so strong I haven't even wet my pants. I can't remember *ever* being this scared before. That time I spent a night in jail at eleven? Yeah, that's bullshit by comparison. It's so goddamn funky being terrified yet not having my heart beat any faster than normal.

Briggs pauses a step inside a doorway long enough to flip a light switch on a wall of grey cinder blocks. A shelf of books, bottles, and jars slides past my vision before he sets me on a somewhat-padded medical table. The rattle of buckles and straps throws my panic into overdrive, but to the outside world, I'm the picture of complete calm. Numbed by the magic, I have no idea what he's doing to me, and the way my head's positioned, I can only see the side of the room where a heating pipe meets a radiator next to a white cabinet, like something out of a horror movie doctor's lab. My eyes won't even move.

A little voice in the back of my head screams for Mommy.

"There, there." Briggs pats me on the cheek—not that I feel it. "Please don't be frightened. You will soon wake up somewhere and forget ever meeting me. I simply cannot have you running off before the memory ritual is over."

Briggs walks off, leaving me alone.

This is so fucking scary, I can't think straight... or blink, move, or even breathe fast. Maybe it wouldn't be so bad to forget this. Holy shit, this could drive me legit nuts in short order. Trying to shift still doesn't do anything. Random pokes and prods of mental energy seem to get me nowhere until I hit something just right and plunge into a psychometric imprint left behind on the table.

My point of view snaps up to stare at the ceiling. I'm no longer numb, and aware of the tightness of straps squeezing my wrists, ankles, and chest. The handsome lighter-haired version of Briggs hovers over whoever I am in the vision, holding a scalpel. A man's voice screams out my mouth as the knife comes down. There's no pain, but the victim lifts his head to stare at his chest being cut open. He gazes on in horror as Briggs removes some internal organ and carelessly lobs it across the room into a sink. Magical light swirls around his hand, and 'my' grotesque wound seals itself closed.

The vision cuts out as the man faints.

Son of a bitch... he's practicing on homeless people. That poor man didn't feel anything, but no way did he walk away from that without serious mental issues. Another flash hits me and drags me into the moment someone watches their left arm amputated above the elbow. Unable to move or scream, I stare at the gradually regenerating arm, watching bloody red roots creep up a length of bone and swell back into muscles. Ugh. No! Stop. I don't want to see this shit.

My mental voice screams into the void as another vision unfurls. The form of a terrified man stretches out below my eyes, his chest cut open. A metal device holds his ribcage wide, exposing the beating heart.

Briggs reaches toward me. "Relax, Mr. Reed. You'll have a new heart in a moment."

The man's scream joins the one in my head, and my vision goes black.

22

EXERCISING RESTRAINT

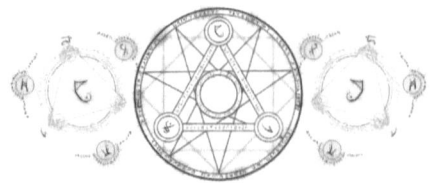

Endless blackness brightens to a blurry haze of dark cinder blocks. Emerson sits near the radiator with his arms handcuffed around the pipe behind him. He's slouched over to the side like a corpse, but he's still breathing. The crinkle of turning pages accompanies Briggs' irritatingly bemused humming, as if he's preparing to bake a fruitcake. He's standing to my left, where I can't turn my head to see.

I daydream about Dad appearing out of thin air and using this asshole's femur as a toothpick. Oh, come on. Little help here? Remember how much I hate being tied up? Yeah, what I pass off as anger is really me being petrified of helplessness. This utter paralysis thing is taking it way beyond.

"Oh, drat," says Briggs. "This is going to require *three* ounces of dediscaria. Silly me."

The squish of soft-soled shoes fades off into the distance, and the creaks and groans of a staircase follow soon after.

I've never wanted anything as much as I want to move. One minute slides into the next, each one more terrifying.

My head fills with mental growling. Seconds pass of pure, concentrated effort and a sense of tightness squeezes around my wrists. It's wearing off! Come on! I manage to blink in super slow motion. The confinement of straps around my ankles and another over my chest seeps into my awareness.

Grr. "I hate being tied up."

Yes! I can talk... sorta. Even if I sound drunk. Yay for half-demon blood.

Emerson moans.

"Can you talk?" I whisper.

He moans again.

"Can you move at all, even blink? Moan once for no, twice for yes."

He moans once.

"Think I'm shrugging the magic off 'cause I'm like all special and stuff." Abject terror morphs into a volatile mixture of rage and determination. Like a switch flipped, I start breathing fast, verging on hyperventilating. My heart slams in my chest. Whoa, Brook. Calm down. Explodey heart *bad!*

Emerson moans again.

"Sorry. Didn't catch that."

He makes a slightly different noise that conveys annoyance.

"Yeah. I agree. I think. Can I kill this shitstain?"

He moans once.

"Aww, please?" I whine, shaking my tied-down body like a five-year-old begging for ice cream.

He moans once.

"Damn. You want him alive?"

He moans twice.

Ten seconds later, it feels like a huge lead blanket disappears from being on top of me. Except for the straps, I can move freely. I lift my head and, sure enough, tight padded leather cuffs secure me in place, though I can probably tear them apart. I'm a little stronger than a plain ol' human. That'll work, but it'll make a buttload of noise. The only thing stopping shitstain from paralyzing me again is not giving him the chance to do it.

I need to be sneaky.

It's difficult to concentrate on fine uses of telekinesis when I'm this pissed off. I manage to undo the buckle on my right wrist, and almost have a heart attack when Briggs walks by overhead. If he comes in here now and catches me moving, I'm screwed. For an average-sized guy, he's got some heavy-ass footsteps. With my right hand loose, it's simple to get my other hand free. I save time by shredding the chest strap away with my claws; same for the belt over my waist and the cuffs around my ankles.

Right as Briggs comes down the stairs, I leap from the table and flatten myself against the wall by the doorway into the room. He breezes in, still humming, and stops short, staring at the shredded restraints and the lack of me.

Before he can twitch, I jump on him from behind, tackling him. The little glass jar in his right hand goes flying, smashing on the concrete floor in a spray of purple dust. I clamp a hand over his mouth so he can't invoke magic. Good for me that I'm far stronger than him; he's not moving that hand. Bad for me that I only weigh like 120. Briggs is plenty strong enough to push himself upright with me on his back. I can't keep him pinned down.

He grabs my wrist with both hands, trying to uncover his mouth, so I wedge my other arm behind his head and cling like a vice while he spins around in circles trying to throw me off.

"Dammit, Emerson... are you sure I can't just kill this guy?"

He moans once.

Briggs yanks and slaps at my arm, screaming via his nose. Good. He knows something's not quite right since he can't pry my grip loose. How's it feel to be pants-stainingly scared, fucko? Anger and frustration cause me to let off a growl more in the range of 400-pound demonic bear than anything that ought to come out of a woman my size.

How can I keep this guy from doing that paralysis bullshit again? The instant his lips are free, I'm screwed. He teeters us close enough to the medical table for me to get a foot on it. I plant my boot and shove, easily flinging us to the floor. Again, I land on top of him, and this time, I try to wrap my legs around his so he can't move. He fights like a beached salmon on crack—one that's being electrocuted. Despite my best effort, we're upright again in moments.

Dammit! *Stop!*

Raw fury and frustration blasts out of my mind. The whole half of the room in front of me glows bright azure. My mind throbs with a strong pulse of energy, along with an unsettling feeling like a ten-foot snot wound around my brain unspools out the middle of my forehead.

Briggs stops moving and falls forward. Again, we hit the ground with me on his back, but he's no longer struggling. Wetness rolls down the hand I've got clamped over his mouth. I pull myself up to look at his face. His eyes have rolled back into his head. Foam's seeping between my fingers and his nose is gushing mucous like a faucet.

Eww.

Everywhere I look turns blue. Oops. My eyes shifted. Wow. I think I just hit him with some kinda psychic blast and derp-slapped his brain. I hurriedly search him and find the handcuff key in his left pants pocket. Hopefully, Briggs will stay tofu-for-brains long enough that I can un-fuck our situation. After unlocking Emerson, I cuff Briggs' hands behind his back. A quick hunt around the outer basement (the part that isn't set up like Dr. Frankenstein's house of love) turns up a nice fat roll of duct tape.

I make sure Briggs isn't in any danger of speaking, and bite the tape off. "What do you think, Em? Twenty passes around his head good enough?"

Emerson moans.

Wait. One moan means no…

"Okay." I pull a length of tape off the spool with a *rip*. "Another ten."

23

FOUR HOURS

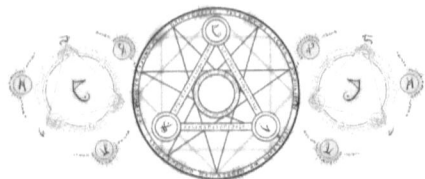

I wind up taking the extra step of giving Briggs a duct tape blindfold. Hey, there's no constitutional right to eyebrows. He's gotta see us to paralyze us, and he's damn lucky I'm using tape to blind him instead of something pointier.

After taping his ankles together, I hurl the half-gone roll across the lab and pull Emerson up off the floor. He's limp as a rag doll, so I set him on the medical table. Nothing I can do for him but wait.

"I can't make that go away any faster..."

Emerson emits a long moan. I cradle his head in both hands and stare into his eyes, trying the thought reading thing again. Ugh. I'm too freaked out and wound up to concentrate. It takes me a few minutes before I get a scrap of his voice in the back of my thoughts ... *call for backup.*

"Backup."

Emerson emits a pair of short moans.

I run upstairs to the living room and peer out the front windows, but the other cops are gone. Guess he hit them with a shorter-term memory loss he didn't need a ritual for. With us, he had to wipe out the whole investigation, not just finding this house. Grr.

Back downstairs, I grab Briggs, haul him off the ground, and put his back to the wall. He's squirming against the handcuffs/tape, so whatever I did to his brain must've worn off already. I suppose that's good since reading scrambled eggs would be a pain in the ass. Eyes closed, I force myself to stop thinking about being terrified, and channel my inner rage.

Remembering how I lost my patience with Eaves, I concentrate on that moment and try to drill into Briggs' mind. My desire to see into his thoughts makes him groan in pain. Guess my psychic blast left him sore. This must be the telepathic equivalent of slapping a sunburn. He's not making *that* much noise, so I don't feel guilty.

Scraps of memory appear and fade in rapid succession. I catch flashes of some of the nazedeh we cleaned up as they had been in life, along with Briggs' thoughts and feelings when he killed them. Within minutes, my jaw's hanging open in complete, appalled disbelief.

"You're not even human…" Metaphorically speaking.

Emerson emits an inquisitive moan.

"This guy… He was using people for medical experiments. Inflicting fatal heart and brain injuries in hopes he could be the first Lifemage to figure out how to fix them fast enough to prevent the person from dying… only it never worked. All his 'subjects' passed away before his magic could repair the damage." I slap Briggs upside the head, not hard enough to break any bones. "What the fuck were you thinking? Even Lifemage magic can't turn a splatter of pudding back into a brain. You know what you were really doing? Every one of your victims got back up hours later as a goddamned zombie."

Briggs squirms and shakes his head no.

"Oh, yes… they did. But not just zombies… nazedeh. You trapped the people you killed in their own dead bodies. Sick bastard. Of course, you targeted the homeless since you thought no one would miss them. What's a few worthless lives if you can learn to save 'real' people?" I snarl, but manage to stop myself before punching him in the gut. Briggs whimpers. "Were you planning to roam the streets so you can be there at the exact moment someone gets shot?"

Ugh. I'm half-tempted to slice this guy open to see if he's got scales under a layer of fake skin.

Emerson moans.

I glance back at him. "How long is Detective Zheng going to remain paralyzed?"

Handcuffs rattle as Briggs sticks out four fingers.

"It's been way longer than four minutes."

Briggs says, "Mmm" past the tape while shaking his head.

"Four hours?!"

He nods.

Emerson moans with sadness.

"Dispel it."

Briggs tries to talk.

"Take the tape off your mouth?" I laugh. "No way. I'm not that stupid. Sorry, Emerson." I pace around Briggs, shaking my head. "I don't trust myself right now to have the self-control necessary to simply knock you out without crushing your skull like an egg. So, sit there and don't even twitch. Not sure what the point of keeping you alive even is. You're a mage, and the law *loves* mages... and you killed like ten people."

Emerson grunts, so I gaze into his thoughts. *Lifemage... prison... medicine.*

"Oh. I guess. You're lucky. Detective Zheng thinks they'll put you to work providing medical services for inmates instead of giving you the death penalty."

Briggs whimpers.

I lean against the medical table next to Emerson and pull out my phone.

"911, what's your emergency?" asks a woman.

"Hi. I need you to send police backup. I'm with Detective Emerson Zheng, and he's been knocked senseless by magic. We've got a suspect in custody, but he's dangerous. Whatever you guys have for dealing with magic criminals, send it..."

"Sweetie, this line isn't for prank calls."

Ugh. "I'm not a kid, dammit. This is serious. One sec." I grab Emerson's ID out of his pocket and read off the badge number before giving the address. "We're all down in the basement. Detective Zheng can't move, and the suspect is momentarily contained."

"All right, sweetie. I'll send a police officer to you. Just stay on the line with me. You're going to be okay. Can you put the detective on the phone?"

I stare at the ceiling in exasperation. How severe would the charges be for bouncing a 911 operator's face off her keyboard a few times? I flip it to speakerphone. "I could physically put him *on* the phone, but that wouldn't help. I told you already, he's been magically paralyzed."

Emerson moans.

"All right. Stay on the line with me until the police arrive, okay?" asks the operator.

"Yeah, sure." I sigh and put an arm around Emerson's back to keep him from falling over. "We'll be right here."

24

DEGREES OF BAD

I'm stretched out on my sofa in a half shirt and short skirt with *Dead Like Me* on in the background. The familiarity of it relaxes me like I've gone 'home' to a safe place. I always had it on in the dorm room unless I was sleeping. Studying, homework, hanging out—always, a constant presence. My attention is primarily focused on Jason Dunn, via the cell phone pressed to my ear. We're both drifting in that 'just got home from work and don't really feel like moving' phase.

"… took them like a half hour to get there. Stupid bitch on the phone thought I was some twelve-year-old playing a joke. The cops who showed up were pretty pissed at her casualness once they saw the situation. I hope that blew back on her and she got read the riot act. Ugh. So anyway, I've gotta go meet the Chief of Police to get some kind of certificate of appreciation for helping them out on that case. That's going to be magnificently awkward."

"Awkward?"

I share the story of how I covered the chief's car with spray-painted penises when I was fifteen. My description of how red the guy's face was has Jason gasping for air between laughs. "I got *so* lucky. He could never prove I did it. Bastard left me in a holding cell for twelve hours with my hands and ankles cuffed, claiming I 'attacked' him because I kicked my boot off a little too forcefully."

"Dick."

I shrug. "Yeah, but I didn't crack. He wanted to scare me into confessing, but I knew he had nothing. It actually wound up helping me since the holding cell had video. A jury would've *loved* watching a 'terrified' fifteen-year old rolling around in handcuffs for hours. They dropped the vandalism charge and Mom agreed not to sue them."

"Handy trick of yours to read people." Jason sighs. "Wish I could do that."

I roll my eyes. "I wish people stopped mistaking me for being too young."

"I don't think you sound like a kid."

Sigh. "But you've seen me. You can put a face to my voice. I get that shit all the goddamned time on the phone."

"You've got a cute voice."

I grin. "I have no underwear on right now. Giving serious thought to going commando tonight. What did you wanna do?"

He grunts, and stammers.

"Getting a bit tight in your jeans?"

"You got my mind going overdrive. I was thinking maybe we could—"

The doorbell rings.

"Ugh. Hang on a sec. Someone's here."

I hop off the couch and plod to the door, still holding the phone to the side of my head. Tracy and Ashley both smile at me when I open it. Tracy's dressed to go outside while Ashley's barefoot and wearing a pink *Little Mermaid* nightgown. Guess that explains why she hit it off so well with Natalie. They're both girly.

"Hey, Brook. Umm. I got a class tonight. Do you mind watching Ash? I should get out at 10:30."

Ashley grins. "Is it still okay if I eat here? We don't have any more Starbucks throw-outs."

I bite my lip. Ugh. Drat. So much for a night on the town plus sex.

"Hey, Jason? How'd you feel about 'dating in,' since I'm apparently watching Ashley tonight?"

"Cool. No problem. Want me to pick anything up on the way?"

"Dinner would be cool." I lean away from the phone and give Ashley a questioning look. "What do you want for dinner?"

"Food," says Ashley with a blank-faced shrug.

I smile at her. "Hmm. Got an itch for Mexican. There's a good place a few blocks from here. Ernesto's. I'll call it in, card it, and you pick it up?"

"Done," says Jason. "See you soon."

I hang up.

"Thanks." Tracy sighs guilt at me. "Sorry for ambushing you like this. Last minute schedule change."

"S'okay. Go forth and nurse or something."

Ashley hugs her mother and darts inside, heading for the sofa while Tracy hurries off down the hall. I close the door and head to the kitchen to grab an Ernesto's menu from the fridge door. I order one of the giant burritos, a six-pack of tacos, some of the black bean and chicken empanadas, and a side of rice n' beans. Should be enough for us all to share… probably with leftovers.

When I flop on the sofa next to her, Ashley looks up. "Sorry for being a pain in the ass."

"You're swearing again," I play-scold. I'm like the *last* person to get on someone for using 'bad words,' even if they are eight.

Ashley sticks her nose in the air. "I summoned you from the pits of hell, and you're upset about a little word?"

"First…" I pounce, grabbing and tickling at her armpits. "I'm not from hell. I grew up in Quakertown."

Peals of laughter drown out the TV for a moment until she's gasping "stop" more than laughing. I relent.

Once she catches her breath, she sticks her tongue out. "Didn't you say you *weren't* from hell?"

I laugh, and poke her in the stomach. "Q-town isn't *that* bad. It's a little boring, but I wouldn't compare it to the Abyss."

She makes a silly face.

"Second, you're too little to swear."

"Did you cuss when you were my age?"

I bite my lip, overacting innocence.

"You did!" She points at me.

"Maybe a little, but never around my mom."

Ashley folds her arms. "You're not my mom. You're my minion."

"Summoning demons and an eight-year-old dropping swears aren't the same thing. There's degrees of bad." I wag my finger at her in a mockery of an angry teacher. "No more uncontained summonings until you're at least fourteen."

"Oh, poop." She raspberries me.

I get the co-op game going, and we spend a few minutes killing jellies in silence before she looks up.

"If you get sent back, I'm gonna summon you again even if I'm not fourteen yet."

"Okay." I wink. "I think I can make an exception in that case."

She grins and leans against me. "You're a cool demon."

I've been promoted. "Not lame?"

Ashley shakes her head. "No, you cut that one monster's head off with your tail. That's cool. Is he gonna be mad at you when he comes back?"

Wow. She *was* paying attention. At least she's treating it like some kind of video game and not reacting like she witnessed a real beheading. I didn't actually *kill* him. Just sent him back to some other dimension. "Ehh, maybe. Dad's probably yelling at them now."

"He was *not* happy." Ashley swipes her hand at the air to further emphasize the 'not.'

"Yeah."

Ashley guides her character down a hallway packed with a small army of glowing red slimes like a master, not even taking a point of damage. "Is your dad really gonna take Miss Diaz flying?"

"Huh, what? Flying?" My eyebrows scrunch together.

"Yeah." Ashley nods. "Miss Diaz said she wanted to ride him real bad."

That's my *father!* She did *not* go there... "Uhh." My voice shakes too much to keep talking.

"What's wrong?" Ashley's face is all innocence.

"Umm... just that flying around is dangerous. If the wrong people see them, they could get in trouble."

"That's stupid. It must be sad to have wings and not be able to use 'em." She holds her arms out. "If I could fly, I'd *always* fly."

Yeah. Flying's the fun part. It's coming back down that sucks.

Ashley grins and settles in against my side, her feet tucked up beneath her. Maybe I could see myself having a kid of my own someday. Whenever Ash looks at me like I'm the greatest person in the world, it's such a weird, warm feeling. She's not even mine. I think I understand how my mother could put up with all my bullshit. Hmm. Maybe I didn't give her near enough of those moments. Think I need to make time to go visit her again.

On second thought... My mind leaps to having a tiny, winged, horned version of myself whizzing around the apartment, shredding the drapes and clawing the shit out of the furniture like a housecat on e-meth. Ehh, maybe I can wait on that. Borrowing the neighbor's kid's good enough for now.

Besides... before I can raise one of my own, I need to do something a little simpler.

I gotta find a way to convince the Shaar'Nath and Elestari to give up on a hundred-thousand-year war.

---

fin

Brooklyn's story continues in Book 3 - The Gate to Oblivion.

Brooklyn Amari doesn't ask for much, only the ability to make it through life without destroying the universe.

Working as a firefighter is her true calling, satisfying her deep, primal draw to the flames. Immunity to burning courtesy of her half-extraplanar ancestry makes her the city's best weapon against disaster of the incendiary kind—not that anyone knows about it. She's trying to keep her nature a secret, since magical creatures aren't allowed inside major population centers… and most people probably wouldn't react well to a demon.

Even a half-demon.

Since her psychic abilities are out of the bag, the Arson Investigation Unit calls on her for all the 'weird ones' no one else wants to touch. When they can't explain an apparent case of spontaneous human combustion, they bring her in to track a deadly arcane arsonist.

She's happy to help, but unfortunately, some not-quite-angels abduct someone she cares for. They need Brooklyn to destroy the mortal world as it's in the way of their interdimensional war—but even if she does what they want, everyone she loves will die.

ACKNOWLEDGMENTS

Thank you for reading The Shadow Collector!

ABOUT THE AUTHOR

Originally from South Amboy NJ, Matthew has been creating science fiction and fantasy worlds for most of his reasoning life. Since 1996, he has developed the "Divergent Fates" world, in which *Division Zero, Virtual Immortality, The Awakened Series, The Harmony Paradox, and the Daughter of Mars series* take place. Along with being an editor at Curiosity Quills press, he has worked in IT and technical support.

Matthew is an avid gamer, a recovered WoW addict, Gamemaster for two custom RPG systems, and a fan of anime, British humour, and intellectual science fiction that questions the nature of reality, life, and what happens after it.

He is also fond of cats.

Visit me online at:
    Facebook: https://www.facebook.com/MatthewSCoxAuthor
    Amazon: https://www.amazon.com/author/mscox
    Pinterest: https://www.pinterest.com/matthewcox10420/
    Goodreads: https://www.goodreads.com/author/show/7712730.Matthew_S_Cox
    Email: mcox2112@gmail.com

OTHER BOOKS BY MATTHEW S. COX

Divergent Fates Universe Novels

Division Zero series

- Division Zero
- Lex De Mortuis
- Thrall
- Guardian
- Harbinger

The Awakened series

- Prophet of the Badlands
- Archon's Queen
- Grey Ronin
- Daughter of Ash
- Zero Rogue
- Angel Descended

Daughter of Mars series

- The Hand of Raziel
- Araphel
- Ghost Black

Virtual Immortality series

- Virtual Immortality
- The Harmony Paradox

Divergent Fates Anthology

(Fiction Novels - Adult)

The Roadhouse Chronicles Series

- One More Run
- The Redeemed
- Dead Man's Number

Faded Skies series

- Heir Ascendant
- Ascendant Unrest
- Ascendant Revolution

Temporal Armistice Series

- Nascent Shadow
- The Shadow Collector
- The Gate to Oblivion

Vampire Innocent series

- A Nighttime of Forever
- A Beginner's Guide to Fangs
- The Artist of Ruin
- The Last Family Road Trip
- The Phantom Oracle

Standalones

- Wayfarer: AV494
- Axillon99
- Chiaroscuro: The Mouse and the Candle
- The Spirits of Six Minstrel Run

- The Far Side of Promise anthology
- Operation: Chimera (with Tony Healey)
- The Dysfunctional Conspiracy (with Christopher Veltmann)

Winter Solstice series (with J.R. Rain)

- Convergence
- Containment
- Catalyst

Alexis Silver series (with J.R. Rain)

- Silver Light
- Deep Silver
- Silver Quarrel

Samantha Moon Origins series (with J.R. Rain)

- New Moon Rising
- Moon Mourning

Vampire For Hire series (with J.R. Rain)

- Moon Master
- Dead Moon

Maddy Wimsey series (with J.R. Rain)

- The Devil's Eye
- The Drifting Gloom

Samantha Moon Case Files series (with J.R. Rain)

- Blood Moon

Immortal Operative series (with J.R. Rain)

- Broken Ice

Young Adult Novels

The Eldritch Heart Series

- The Eldritch Heart
- The Cursed Crown

Evergreen Series

- Evergreen
- The World That Remains

Standalones

- Caller 107
- The Summer the World Ended
- Nine Candles of Deepest Black
- The Forest Beyond the Earth
- Out of Sight
- Evergreen

Middle Grade Novels

Tales of Widowswood series

- Emma and the Banderwigh
- Emma and the Silk Thieves
- Emma and the Silverbell Faeries

- Emma and the Elixir of Madness
- Emma and the Weeping Spirit

Standalones

- Citadel: The Concordant Sequence
- The Cursed Codex
- The Menagerie of Jenkins Bailey
- Sophie's Light

www.ingramcontent.com/pod-product-compliance
Lightning Source LLC
Chambersburg PA
CBHW020619180626
46810CB00007B/2854